A PROPERLY
UNHAUNTED PLACE

ALSO BY WILLIAM ALEXANDER

Goblin Secrets

Ghoulish Song

Ambassador

Nomad

A PROPERLY
UNHAUNTED PLACE

William Alexander

Illustrated by
Kelly Murphy

MARGARET K. McELDERRY BOOKS
New York London Toronto Sydney New Delhi

MARGARET K. McELDERRY BOOKS
An imprint of Simon & Schuster Children's Publishing Division
1230 Avenue of the Americas, New York, New York 10020
MARGARET K. McELDERRY BOOKS is a trademark of Simon & Schuster, Inc.
For information about special discounts for bulk purchases, please contact Simon & Schuster Special Sales at 1-866-506-1949 or business@simonandschuster.com.
The Simon & Schuster Speakers Bureau can bring authors to your live event. For more information or to book an event, contact the Simon & Schuster Speakers Bureau at 1-866-248-3049 or visit our website at www.simonspeakers.com.
Book design by Sonia Chaghatzbanian and Irene Metaxatos
The text for this book was set in Horley Old Style MT Std.
The illustrations for this book were rendered in pencil.
Manufactured in the United States of America
0717 FFG
First Edition
10 9 8 7 6 5 4 3 2 1
Library of Congress Cataloging-in-Publication Data
Names: Alexander, William (William Joseph), 1976– author. | Murphy, Kelly, 1977– illustrator.
Title: A properly unhaunted place / William Alexander ; illustrated by Kelly Murphy.
Description: First edition. | New York : Margaret K. McElderry Books, [2017] | Summary: "In a world full of ghosts, Rosa and Jasper live in the only unhaunted town—but must spring to action when they realize the ghosts are lying in wait to take the town back"—Provided by publisher.
Identifiers: LCCN 2016031757 (print) | LCCN 2016059961 (eBook) | ISBN 9781481469159 (hardcover) | ISBN 9781481469173 (eBook)
Subjects: | CYAC: Ghosts—Fiction. | Haunted places—Fiction. | Libraries—Fiction. | Books and reading—Fiction. | Mothers and daughters—Fiction. | Supernatural—Fiction.
Classification: LCC PZ7.A3787 Pro 2017 (print) | LCC PZ7.A3787 (eBook) | DDC [Fic]—dc23 LC record available at lccn.loc.gov/2016031757

para mis sobrinos
Suzanna Moxie
y Brady Guillermo

—W. A.

A PROPERLY
UNHAUNTED PLACE

ROSA AND HER MOTHER MOVED INTO A BASEMENT
apartment underneath the Ingot Public Library.

"This is nice," Mom said. "This will do fine."

Rosa said nothing. She said it loudly. Rosa was not
impressed with the basement apartment, or the library
above it, or the town of Ingot. She missed their old place
in the city. She missed having windows. She missed
looking through those windows to see a place that was
not Ingot.

Her new bedroom was bigger than her old one,
but without any outside view the room still seemed
smaller. Someone had tried to fix this by installing a
fake window frame and painting beautiful landscapes

of forests and lakes on the plaster behind it.

Rosa closed real curtains over the fake view.

This was not home. She could unpack her stuff and spread it around, but that would not make it home. This was just an underground room she happened to be haunting.

Rosa went back into the living room. She didn't find much life in there, either. Mom lay flopped across the couch, which was in an awkward place. It blocked the way to the kitchen. Rosa wanted to shove it into its proper place, but it *properly* belonged in the city, in their old apartment, directly adjacent to the huge central library. Rosa couldn't shove it that far. She couldn't even shove it away from the kitchen because her mother had fallen asleep on it.

Mom looked defeated. She also looked content with her defeat, and that was worse.

Rosa climbed over her mother, who stayed asleep— or at least pretended to sleep—and left the apartment. She didn't bring her tool belt. She didn't even know where it was. That didn't matter, though. Not here.

She went upstairs to explore the Ingot Public Library.

Nice old building. Rosa closed her eyes and smelled the familiar, musty, dusty smell of old books given time to think. Then she opened her eyes and let herself wander into odd corners and unusual nooks. That quickly brought her somewhere she wasn't supposed to be.

"This is Special Collections, dear," said a woman with wispy hair, white gloves, and aggressive eyebrows. "This is where we keep *very old* books, maps, and historical records. You need *permission* to be here. You need to sign the *form* on the *clipboard*. And children aren't allowed at all, even if they do sign the form on the clipboard. *Children's* books are through that door, down the hall, and in the far corner. *Please* don't touch anything on your way there." Her voice tasted like honey dribbled over raw rhubarb.

"I live here," Rosa said. She did not want this to be true, but it was, and she felt indignant to have to explain it. "We just moved in. My mother is the new appeasement specialist." Librarian appeasement specialists always lived inside their libraries, or at least next to their libraries. They had to be on call at all hours.

"Ah," the other librarian said. She took the time to make eye contact now. "I see. Though I'm not at all sure why such an esteemed specialist has chosen to work here, in Ingot."

"She just needed a change," Rosa said.

Silence stretched thin between them.

"Ah," the librarian finally said. "Well then. Hello. Welcome. I'm Mrs. Jillynip. Pleased to meet you. But please don't come and go through this part of the collection. Not without gloves."

Mrs. Jillynip went away without bothering to learn Rosa's name. Then she watched Rosa sideways to make sure she didn't touch any of the maps. That made Rosa want to touch maps. She wanted to jump up and down on a big pile of maps. But she didn't. Instead she tried to leave by way of a spiral staircase in the corner of the room.

"Not there!" Mrs. Jillynip snapped. Then she took a breath and tried to be more civil. "Please don't ever go up there."

"Why not?" Rosa asked.

"Because nothing's up there. And it isn't safe. The whole staircase might come down. Then the Historical Society would be angry with you. Plus you'll probably break both of your legs. Children's books are *that way*."

Rosa turned around and went that way. She passed through the children's section. It had more dusty, creepy, glass-eyed stuffed animals than actual books, so she left to explore the rest of her new library. She noticed all the places where haints, ghosts, revenants, specters, the spirits of the living, and the spirits of the dead would collect themselves if this building stood anywhere other than Ingot. She spotted all the little things that would probably offend them, or enrage them, or send them howling in between the bookshelves in the very small hours of the night if this were any other library in any other town.

Ingot was not haunted. Ingot was the only unhaunted place that Rosa had ever heard of. The Ingot Public Library did not need an appeasement specialist. It had nothing to appease—nothing but Rosa.

She moved unappeased through the library stacks until she found the public bathroom. The sink fixtures inside were all copper, polished in some places and stained green in others. Each mirror had a small shelf underneath it, just like mirrors are always supposed to have, but the shelves stood empty. No coins. No pebbles. No candle stubs. A candle would have been especially helpful. Ghosts could use them to rest, or to pass between boundaries. Lit candles could also make nasty smells disappear, and would have been helpful in this particular bathroom.

Rosa washed her hands. Then she took a pebble from her pocket and set it on the mirror shelf. This was a decent way to say thanks to a mirror—and to anything likely to lurk inside a mirror. It was also a way to greet lost relatives.

"Hi Dad," she said, even though he wasn't there.

A blonde girl pushed the bathroom door open. She gave Rosa a funny look. Rosa ignored her intensely and left the bathroom. She needed to leave the building. She hurried through the front lobby and half-ran beneath a portrait of a man with a long, elaborate mustache—Bartholomew Theosophras Barron, founder of Ingot Town. Mr. Barron's painted eyes looked into the distance in a self-important way. They didn't follow Rosa as she rushed outside.

She went without her tool belt, without matches, chalk, or salt, without any proof of her family profession but another pebble in her pocket and a little copper medallion of Catalina de Erauso, Rosa's patron librarian, around her neck. The medallion showed de Erauso holding a sword above the Latin inscription MEMENTO MORTUIS. *"Remember the dead."* There was nothing special about the pebble.

It felt wrong to leave the building without her tool belt. Rosa left anyway. She sat on the library steps and decided she was angry. She liked that decision, even though she knew it wasn't right. Sadness slowed her down. It made the air feel thick to move through and heavy to carry in her lungs. But anger was fuel she could use to move faster. She would rather be mad—at Mom for the move, and for taking a job that didn't really need her, and for needing such a clean and brutal break away from their proper work. She would rather be mad at Ingot for its odd, unnatural emptiness of everyone except for the living. So she decided that she was.

The town stretched out in front of her. She could see most of it from here. Old houses clustered close together, some in good repair and others run-down and peeling. Mountains surrounded Ingot on all sides like the rim of a bowl or a bucket.

Bright green light flashed briefly in the foothills. Rosa stared at the spot where that green flash wasn't anymore. Then a knight in full armor came striding down the sidewalk, and she stared at him instead.

2

JASPER WORE HIS SQUIRE COSTUME AND FOLLOWED
his dad to the fairgrounds. He would rather have worn
a T-shirt and jeans, and changed into this fashionable
burlap outfit *after* they arrived at the fairgrounds, but
Jasper's father liked to tour around town in full armor—a
walking, talking, extremely public ad for the Renaissance
Festival.

Jasper did not enjoy strutting around as an anachronistic advertisement, but his father did. Very much.
The man stood tall and took up space around him while
he walked, armor clinking like a cowboy's spurs. He
drew all eyes to himself. Jasper moved in his shadow,
haunted his footsteps, and was perfectly okay with the

fact that knights got more attention than their squires.

A girl came running at them from the library steps. Jasper didn't recognize her, even though she looked to be about his age—which was eleven as of last Tuesday. He knew every other eleven-year-old in Ingot. He didn't know her. But she seemed to recognize both of them.

Jasper's father paused and removed his helmet.

"How may we be of service?" he asked. His voice was a bass drum with a fake British accent. He spoke every word as a beat meant to carry, a sound you could feel in the bones of your face. Jasper could always hear his father's voice from elsewhere in their large house. It passed through walls, doors, and headphones.

The girl's look of wonder and recognition drained right out of her.

"You're not a ghost," she said, clearly disappointed.

"I am not," Dad agreed. "Ingot is not known for hauntings. I impersonate Sir Morien, Black Knight of Arthur's court and table. My squire and I are bound for the Renaissance Festival—the largest and most splendid celebration of its kind to be found anywhere in the world."

Jasper waved. Sir Dad produced a brochure and held it out in one gauntleted hand.

The girl didn't take it. She crossed her arms and

looked him over critically. "King Arthur lived in the fifth century—*if* he lived at all. Which he probably didn't. Your getup looks like something fifteenth-century-ish."

Oh no, Jasper thought. *He found another one already.* They hadn't even reached the festival yet, and Dad had already stirred up an argument of historical nitpickery with a total stranger. Jasper's parents had spent all morning arguing over the word "caddis" and whether it meant cobwebs or belly button lint. Either way, doctors used to use the stuff like Band-Aids to staunch small wounds. Both parents had agreed on that part, at least. But they still spent all morning bouncing linty and spidery theories back and forth across the kitchen table. Mom was very nearly late for the opening ceremony at the fairgrounds—and Mom was the queen, so she couldn't be late. Jasper had tried to convince his knightly father to skip their walk around town, but Dad insisted. "We must awaken sleepy Ingot and remind them that our summer revels have begun," he had said, even though everyone already knew. The festival was huge, and pretty much the only thing that happened here.

Sir Dad grinned, delighted to have the historical accuracy of his costume called into question. "Well noticed. And clearly well-read."

"I've always lived in libraries," the girl said. "And I've read about a Black Knight who tied people to trees, but never . . ."

". . . but never a *black* knight?" Dad finished. His smiling teeth looked bright beside his dark skin. Dad always used extra-whitening toothpaste.

Here we go, Jasper thought. *He loves this part.*

"Clearly, you have only ever seen *abridged* versions of the Arthurian tales. Sir Morien was the son of a valiant English knight and a Moorish lady of North Africa. His deeds of valor were well documented. In the fifteenth century. And anyone who can recognize the age of my armor in an offhand way should obviously accompany us, so this admission ticket is yours to spend."

He added a ticket to the brochure and held out his hand again. She hesitated, then took both.

Sir Dad put on his helmet and continued to march down the sidewalk.

Jasper and the girl followed him. They crossed Main Street and headed south on Isabelle Road, toward the fairgrounds.

"Hey," Jasper said without the accent he would be using later.

"Hey," said the girl. "What's your name?"

"Jasper Chevalier. Yours?"

"Rosa Ramona Díaz. I just moved here."

"Into the library?"

"Yes," Rosa said. "Into the *basement* of the library. We don't have any windows. I'm pretty sure that violates housing code. Apartments are supposed to have windows. Maybe I can force them to move us somewhere else." She dug a pebble from her pocket and rolled it around between fingertips.

"It's a nice old building," Jasper said, just to say something nice. "Not enough comics, though. Or science fiction. How come you've always lived in libraries?"

"My mom is Athena Díaz." She paused and glanced at him. Maybe he was supposed to recognize that name. He didn't. "The appeasement specialist."

"Ah," he said.

"The ghost appeasement specialist," she added.

Jasper felt suddenly, desperately curious. Until that moment he had only asked questions to make a conversation happen, but now he asked because he actually wanted to know. "Your mom is a ghost hunter?"

Rosa sighed. "No. I mean yes, she is. And she's the best at it. 'Hunting' just isn't the right word."

"But she does banish ghosts, right?"

"No!" Rosa said, loud enough to make Sir Morien pause and glance back at them. She lowered her voice

down from a shout. "Not banishment. Never banishment. Pretty much the opposite. Hauntings don't just
go away. Or at least they shouldn't."

This topic was clearly upsetting. *I should stop asking
about it*, Jasper thought. Whenever folk moved to Ingot
from elsewhere, they tended not to talk about why. It
usually involved a haunting, one that they really didn't
want to confront, so instead they all came to a place
without ghosts.

But he couldn't stop himself from asking. "What
did your mom do, if not hunt or banish?"

"Appease. Calmed ghosts down if they got upset.
Showed proper respect to keep them from getting upset.
Kept really nasty ones distracted, and found a proper
place for them to be. Like the combustible ones. She'd
just settle those down in the fireplace. But she wouldn't
ever banish them. Libraries need to be haunted."

"Why?" Jasper asked.

Rosa wasn't sure how to answer, because it was just
obviously true.

"Ghosts are everywhere," she said. "Usually.
Though you might not notice them unless you annoy
them. But hauntings just build up in some places. And
those places need to have appeasement specialists on
hand."

"Like libraries."

"Yes. Like libraries. Whenever you open an old book you read it along with everyone else who's ever read that same book. You're supposed to. Hauntings don't end. Ghosts don't ever just go away."

"Except here," Jasper pointed out.

"Except here," Rosa sighed. Her words tumbled together before, but now she slowed right down and fiddled with the pebble in her hand. "So Mom will just handle the interlibrary loans here. All the books that people complain about. The ones they think are too haunted. They'll pass through here to get unhaunted. Disinfected. Which is horrible. It shouldn't even be possible. But Mom will make sure it happens anyway. That's her only job now. Every library has to have its specialist—even if it doesn't have any ghosts. Why doesn't it? Why *aren't* there ghosts in Ingot?"

"There just aren't," Jasper said. "I don't know why. Nobody does."

The two walked in silence for a bit and listened to Sir Morien's armor clink, clink, clink ahead of them. Rosa looked around.

"It's nice," she said, with effort. "The town looks . . . comfortable. Homey. Not uncanny. Canny."

They reached the edge of town. It didn't take very long to get there.

"The fairgrounds are this way," Jasper said, pointing

off to the right. "You can see the gates and some of the pavilions from here. And that's my house, over the other way." He pointed left.

A wooden sign of a carved and painted horse hung above the mailbox at the end of the driveway.

"You live on a horse farm?" Rosa asked.

"I do," Jasper said.

"I always thought the words 'horse' and 'farm' sounded funny together. Like horses are plants and you grow a crop of them out of the ground."

"Oh, they are," Jasper said, playing along. "Horses hatch out of pumpkins. Didn't you know that? It's why we carve the pumpkins in October. We have to let all the little horses out."

"Makes sense," Rosa said. Then she got quiet.

"Why do we *really* carve pumpkins?" he asked, because she clearly knew why.

"To give wandering spirits a place to keep warm," she said. "They can rest inside lanterns. Or move through the candles to get somewhere else."

Sir Dad led them off the road and across a long stretch of grassy, unpaved parking lot. Nearby fairgoers climbed out of cars and into costumes. Sir Dad paused to help parents push a unicorn-shaped stroller out of the mud. Then he moved through the steady stream of people that flowed toward the festival gates. He waved and shouted enthusiastic greetings. He paused to answer skeptical questions, and to insist—again, over and over again—that knights of North Africa did indeed ride through European legends of chivalry. *I am Sir Morien*, he said with every armored step. *I have a place in this history*. And he made that place as large as he could manage.

All of that was fine and grand, but Jasper still wished he could help from some unseen distance. He would rather be backstage, hidden and secret, than standing in a spotlight—or even standing next to his father's spotlight. But it was summertime in Ingot, and summer belonged to the festival. Squire Jasper had his duty to do. So he walked with Rosa in Sir Morien's wake.

3

THE FESTIVAL STOOD AT THE FAR END OF THE field, up against trees and the base of the foothills. Rosa followed Sir Morien and Jasper the Squire though the grassy parking lot, and then up to towering plaster gates pretending to be stone. She handed over her admission ticket and got her hand stamped with a little pink skull and crossbones.

Centuries smacked into each other on the other side of the gate. Wandering minstrels played classic rock on mandolins. A barista called out the virtues of Ye Olde Cappuccinos and promised to draw Jolly Rogers in the milky foam. Dozens of people wore eye patches, striped breeches, and stuffed parrots awkwardly stapled to their shoulders.

"This is Pirate Week," Jasper explained, unnecessarily.

"Speak the language of the realm," Sir Morien reminded him.

Jasper shifted his vowels around. "Ahem. The fairgrounds are rife with buccaneers."

Sir Morien knelt down to Rosa's height. "I hope that you enjoy our festival, and that our revels make you feel more welcome here in Ingot. I must excuse myself to prepare for the afternoon joust, but my son and squire can provide you with a tour. He should nonetheless remember that he is charged with passing the hat and collecting tips during the belly dancers' show."

Rosa smirked, but she also curtsied. "My thanks for your welcome, good Sir Knight. I wish you luck in the lists."

He laughed a mighty laugh. "Lady Rosa," he said, and then went striding away through the crowd.

"Thanks for that," Jasper whispered, out of accent and out of character again. "He loves it when people play along."

Rosa shrugged. "No big deal. I'm used to showing proper respect in odd circumstances. And you don't have to give the tour if you don't feel like it. I can just wander around."

"Yes, I do," Jasper said. "I have to offer, anyway."

Rosa didn't know if she even wanted a tour. She looked around her and tried to decide.

Ladies dressed as gypsies offered to tell fortunes.

A wagon full of pirates rolled by and loudly rolled their every R.

Muck jugglers juggled lumps of dried muck.

It was all a huge game of pretend. Some people pretended *hard*, as if this game mattered more than anything. Others played along halfway, wearing piratic shirts over jeans and sneakers. Most were just tourists and spectators, here to watch the game rather than play along. The place made weird, cacophonous echoes of history that reminded Rosa of a library book—a very old one, with centuries of attention soaked into every page, but with several of those pages torn out and glued back together in haphazard order. That thought hurt more than she knew how to handle.

"You okay there?" Jasper asked.

"Fine," Rosa said. She didn't want to feel sad. She was done with sad. Sadness was stillness, and she wanted to be moving.

A staged duel broke out between two performers. Rosa watched them strut, boast, and swing at each other. She winced. So did Jasper.

"Those two aren't very good," she said.

"No," Jasper agreed. "Sloppy. They never rehearse."

"And they don't even notice when their circles overlap."

Catalina de Erauso, Rosa's patron librarian, had written books about duelists and geometry in sixteenth-century Spain: *To hold a sword is to become the center of a circle, that most perfect and flawless form. Its circumference is the farthest reach of your blade. Those who intrude across that boundary are a danger to you, and in danger from you. Maintain your awareness of your circle and its edge.*

Jasper looked at her, surprised. "Do you fence?"

"A little," Rosa said. "Most specialists do. We need to make and break boundaries a lot."

She didn't explain further. Appeasement specialists usually studied fencing right alongside circles, boundaries, and dangerous geometry. Rosa and her mother used to practice for fun. They used to duel whenever they got annoyed with each other and needed to vent without words. But they didn't anymore. And Rosa didn't want to think about the family business, or how little it mattered in Ingot. She wanted to set fire to how that made her feel, burn those feelings as fuel, and keep moving.

She also wanted to be somewhere else, away from the two duelists who didn't know how to duel.

"Let's go," Rosa said. "I think I would like a tour."

4

JASPER HELD OUT BOTH ARMS TO ENCOMPASS THE whole festival. Pride and embarrassment wrestled inside his chest, equally matched. He did love this place, but he also felt mortified to be the center of attention—even just the center of one person's attention.

He took refuge behind an accent and began.

"Welcome to the Ingot Renaissance Festival, the largest and most magnificent of its kind. The Fest began when a small band of history buffs elected to spend their summer jousting at each other. Both of my parents were among them, and supplied the horses from our family farm."

They passed the Mousetrap Stage, where Goose Lady

was halfway through her standup routine. Ferdinand the gander perched on her head and flapped his wings to prompt applause.

"Those few friends taught themselves how to joust by tilting at straw dummies. They took this seriously enough to get good at it, and soon they could spear rings the size of teacups with a twelve-foot lance at full gallop. One founder, Nell MacMinnigan, learned smithy work and taught herself how to make armor so that they would be less likely to accidentally kill each other. Nell should be working at her forge today, so we can stop by and say hello. Mind the tortoise." They stepped wide around Handisher the tortoise, who wore livery in the queen's colors draped over his shell. "Handisher roams our festival at will. Most of the stalls sell turtle treats in little paper cups for anyone who wants to feed him. Where was I?"

"Nell the smith," Rosa prompted.

"Right. Nell's armor and weapons got fancier and shinier. The weekend jousts became more of a show. Crowds began to gather. The costumes and armor were expensive, so they started to sell tickets. And lemonade. The festival expanded from there. It began as a summertime hobby, and now it's immense. The lemonade stall is still here, next to the Tacky Tavern. We can take refreshment there if you like."

"No thanks," Rosa said.

Jasper couldn't tell if she was enjoying herself or not. She looked at every single thing as though hoping to spot something else hiding behind it.

They passed the Waxworks, where the air smelled thick and sweet, and watched Duncan the candlemaker dip handmade wicks into a vat of bubbling beeswax. He hung thin amber candles from a row of iron hooks to dry.

"There used to be another wax stall across the way," Jasper said, his voice low. "Fantastical Candles. They sold sculpted wax castles and glittery unicorns. They also made beer steins full of wax that looked like beer, and coffee mugs full of darker wax that looked like coffee. Bad idea, I thought. Candles shouldn't pretend to be drinkable. That's an invitation to a mouthful of hot pain. But the beer steins and coffee mugs sold pretty well. Anyway, Duncan here, the master candlemaker, absolutely *hated* Fantastical Candles. He drove them away with the overwhelming force of his disapproval. Duncan never drops character—not ever—and he's fully devoted to the absolute, several-centuries-old authenticity of his craft."

Rosa admired a few huge candles as tall as herself. "These would be useful in a properly haunted place."

"Touch them not," the candlemaker growled over one shoulder.

Rosa already had. She backed away and tried to rub wax residue from her fingertips.

Jasper sighed. The candlemaker's devotion to his work often stopped him from actually selling any of it.

"What's that place over there?" Rosa asked.

"Mermaid Lagoon," he said. "Let's go say hello. The mermaids won't answer us, not if they stay in character. They'll just sing and wave."

He led the way around shrubs and stones, over a small wooden bridge, and down a dirt path to the lagoon. It looked like a low-budget zoo exhibit, a cement enclosure trying very hard to seem like a natural habitat. Three mermaids lounged at the far side of the pool, their legs tucked into brightly painted rubber tails. Jasper waved. They waved back. Spectators wandered through to gawk and toss coins in the water. A jewelry stall beside the path sold necklaces, seashells, and very old coins.

Rosa watched the lagoon with a critical eye. "They don't look very much like mermaids. Or undines. Or nymphs. Or any other kind of water spirit that I know about."

"You've seen some?" Jasper tried to ask casually. He tried to hold down his intense curiosity. It made his voice crack. He cleared his throat.

"Just one," she said. "Freshwater. Lived in a big

public fountain outside our library, and mostly behaved. Mostly. As long as she got steady offerings of coins and wishes."

"Did she grant wishes?" Jasper asked.

"No," Rosa said. "She ate them. Ate the coins, too, but I think she found them less nutritious than the wishes. And she looked different. Not so . . ."

"Pretty?"

"*Flirty*. She was pretty. She had really long arms, though. Two elbows at least. Sometimes three. I never learned her name. Maybe she didn't have one. Maybe she ate it already."

They stood and listened to the fake mermaids sing. Rosa rolled her pebble around in her hand. Jasper tried to decide where to go next. He was about to suggest the Human Dice Game, where they could watch acrobatic comedians tumble inside huge wicker cubes. But then he heard scuffling noises and a louder, sharper sound, which he finally recognized as screaming.

5

ONE MOMENT SPED UP. LOTS OF NOISE AND movement crowded into it, all together, all at once.

The next moment slowed right down.

Rosa saw a beast come loping out of the forest and into the Mermaid Lagoon. She couldn't see it clearly. Sunlight bent around the thing as though reluctant to touch it.

She reached for her tool belt. It wasn't there. She had left all the tools of her trade in the library basement, packed away in one of many cardboard boxes. She didn't have chalk, salt, or a source of fire. She didn't have her pocketknife or favorite marble. The marble wasn't actually good for anything, but it was

her favorite and she carried it with her, always. Except today. She wasn't supposed to need any of it today. Today she had a small rock and a medallion of Patron Catalina.

The medallion felt suddenly and uncomfortably cold as the haunted thing approached.

Most of the beast was a mountain lion—or at least it used to be. Now it was something else. An antlered deer skull sat where its head used to be.

The beast loped forward, half upright on hind legs. Its forelimbs dangled loose as if forgotten. The antlers moved instead. They moved with pointed, prehensile, grasping intention as though they properly belonged on the body of a crab or a spider.

I need a circle, Rosa thought. She needed to draw a line in the dirt, an unbroken line, one that would set her apart. She needed a barrier to create a separate place with separate rules inside. But she didn't have salt. She didn't have chalk. And the hard packed dirt didn't notice when she tried to draw a line with her shoe.

Rosa needed to make a circle, but she had none of her tools because there were no ghosts in Ingot. Everyone knew that. This beast wasn't supposed to be here. It wasn't supposed to *be*.

Coin-throwing spectators all ran screaming. The three mermaids couldn't run, not with their legs stuck inside their costume tails. And Rosa didn't run. She stood, stared, and scuffed at the ground with her foot.

The skull-headed thing leaned forward as though sniffing with a nose it didn't have. It climbed up onto the wall of the lagoon, reaching with stretched antler tips. Jasper could smell it. It smelled like blood tasted after you bit the tip of your tongue.

He desperately wished for a sword, or a spear, or a jousting lance. Or even just a stick. A chair. Anything. He needed to insist on some distance between the beast and everyone else, everyone living. He needed to do something. He needed to move.

Rosa moved first. She grabbed a spool of wire from the jewelry stall and threw down a wide loop of the stuff. Then she stepped inside that circle and pulled him in. Jasper shivered. It felt like the air held in that loop no longer mixed with the air outside. He still heard shouting, but it sounded far away, like a TV playing in another room.

Rosa took the pebble from her pocket, aimed, and threw. It clacked against the skull with a hollow sound.

The beast turned. It moved closer to the circle. Antlers grasped at the boundary. One paw touched the very edge.

Green light flashed from that point of contact. The beast held up its head as though silently roaring. Then it ran back through the trees and was gone.

Jasper watched the beast run. He wondered how half a mountain lion could still move so fast.

"It crossed water," Rosa said to herself, very softly. "Didn't mind getting paws wet in the lagoon, either. That narrows it down."

"What happened?" Jasper whispered.

Rosa bent down to examine the wire loop. A pale green patina covered the spot where the antler tip had touched and flinched away.

"It burned itself," she said. "Burned against the circle I made. Even though it wasn't much of a circle. Just a wonky thing I tossed together."

"What happened?" Jasper asked again.

Rosa rubbed the green-stained wire between two fingers. "Something needed new clothes to wear, so it squished a dead deer skull to a dead cat and then came down from the hills. The mountain lion might not have been dead, though. Not yet. I noticed it breathing. Which is kind of awful to think about. But it did lose its *original* head, so hopefully it doesn't feel much pain. I suppose that depends where the old head ended up."

Jasper stared at the girl who stared at the wire and

spoke calmly of missing heads and half-lions.

"What happened?" he asked, one more time.

Rosa looked at him then, and she looked overjoyed.

"A haunting," she said.

6

ROSA FELT HER SENSE OF TIME RETURN TO NORMAL. Breath and heartbeat fell back into their usual rhythms. Each moment handed off "now" to the next.

The trio of mermaids hurried to get out of the water and out of their immobilizing tails.

Jasper continued to watch the trees, his earlier curiosity sharpened by fear and wonder.

"Have you ever seen anything like that before?" he asked.

"No," Rosa told him. "I really haven't tangled with rearranged wildlife before. But I did handle a pigeon-eating statue once. He'd swallow everything but the wings, stick those mangled wings back together, and then convince them to fly all by themselves. The statue got loose in our library, along with a whole flock of his birdless wings. Mom was on call at another branch, so I had to chase them out myself."

"You are a deeply unsettling person," Jasper said. "Statues move where you come from?"

"Sometimes," she said. "Not usually. But they are heavy, sculpted memories, so they're pretty much always haunted. And if any of the restless kind see my mother coming, they move very fast and in the opposite direction."

She stepped outside the wire circle, dug out her phone, and pushed the only number in the "favorite" menu. *Mom needs to be here. Mom needs to see this.* But Mom didn't answer, not after several rings. Rosa stuffed the phone back in her pocket.

Jasper left the circle. The look on his face completely changed in that moment.

"We should finish up the tour," he said, distracted. "Then I need to get to the belly dancer's show. I'm supposed to pass the hat."

"Excuse me?" Rosa couldn't quite believe that sideshow tips had taken sudden precedence over ghostly things. "What about the haunting?"

"Ingot isn't haunted," Jasper said. "I wish it was sometimes. But it isn't."

"Okay," Rosa said. She slowed down and spoke carefully. "Do you remember what just happened?"

"Of course," he said. "Rabid mountain lion. Scary. They don't usually come all the way down here."

She glanced at the mermaids—now just a trio pulling blue jeans over bathing suits. They seemed annoyed, but not afraid, and they left as soon as they had pants on.

Rosa scooped up the wire and twisted off a piece. "Your memory worked a whole lot better inside that circle. Give me your wrist."

"Right or left?" he asked.

"Doesn't matter."

He held out his left arm. She looped some wire around his wrist and twisted the ends together to make a hasty bracelet.

"Tell me what you saw," she asked him. "Tell me what came out of those woods."

"A mountain lion," he said, but then his eyes sharpened. "*Part* of one. With a deer skull for a head. And the antlers moved around in ways that they really aren't supposed to."

"Whew," Rosa said. "Good. Please don't take that bracelet off. Not even to shower. You might forget to put it back on."

Jasper blinked a couple of times, his head still fuzzy

from overlapping memories that didn't quite agree. "Why did I . . . ?"

"No idea," she told him. "Maybe Ingot is haunted and always has been. That'd be nice. But maybe ghosts keep themselves hidden here. No echoes, no memories. I can't think why they would do that, though. Have you seen other rearranged wildlife before? That you can remember, anyway?"

"No," he said. "And I've spent every single summer in this field. I've got a picture of Dad on horseback with a lance in one arm and month-old me cradled in the other."

Rosa tried to call her mother again. "Pick up, pick up, pick up, pick up. I don't even know where she packed our tool belts. And she should be here. She's the specialist. Pick up!" Rosa needed her mother to stop napping beneath a building that had no need or use for her. She needed her to get back to work, to become herself again, ablaze with skill and vital purpose. She needed both of them to be in motion. But Mom didn't pick up. Rosa put away her phone. Then she clapped her hands together in a *let's get to work* sort of way. "Right. Okay. If it comes back, it'll probably follow the same path it took before—which will bring it here, to the lagoon. Haunted things follow habits. So we need to work a little appeasement on this spot. And I don't have my tool belt. Do you know where we can find matches and a pocketknife? And salt? Lots and lots of salt."

"Tacky Tavern," Jasper suggested. "People buy roasted turkey legs for the rugged, barbarian authenticity of gnawing meat from a large bone. But the legs are always overcooked and kinda tasteless, so they go through a lot of paper salt packets."

"Perfect! Do you have time to help before you need to go belly dance, or whatever it is you're doing later?"

Jasper glared, cranked up his accent, and dropped his voice to sound more like his father. "Yes, Lady Rosa the fancy special ghost-herding person. I can spare you a little of my time."

"Excellent," she said. "To the tavern!" It felt splendid to have something important to do, and to know how to do it. She held tight to that feeling and the momentum it gave her.

They left the lagoon. Jasper pulled a chain across the path behind them. A wooden sign dangled from it and read CLOSED in fancy calligraphy.

"Our apologies!" he shouted at fairgoers trying to head down that way. "The mermaids are enjoying their lunch break, lest they become so ravenous that they devour the names and wishes of everyone who passes by. Best keep away!"

"Good thinking," Rosa said.

The two of them dodged around a gaggle of theatrically drunk buccaneers and headed for the Tacky Tavern.

Rosa's phone rang.

Jasper held back to give Rosa a privacy bubble.

She soon raised her voice and broke the bubble.

"A skull stuck to a mountain lion! Great big antlers that moved around like jointed fingers!"

Jasper took another step away and tried not to listen too obviously.

"No, Mom, our first duty *isn't* to the library. Not right this very now it isn't. How can you just sit there and unpack while something sticks pieces of a wild beast together and menaces fake mermaids?"

Her voice got louder. She drew attention to herself. Jasper wished he could make a circle around Rosa to give her somewhere else to be, a separate place that wasn't so very public and alarming. But no one else seemed to be especially alarmed.

He fiddled with his copper bracelet. The metal felt cold against his wrist. The haunted beast sat cold in his memory.

"I *know* I can handle this, but—" Rosa stopped. Jasper watched her give up. She mumbled a few responses to whatever her mother told her on the other end of the line. "Yes. Yes. Sure. But are you wearing your patron medallion? Right now? Would you put it on, please? Just humor me. Okay. Bye." She put the phone back in her pocket.

Festival crowds continued to happily flow. Handisher the tortoise went plodding by.

Jasper closed the distance between them.

"She didn't argue," Rosa whispered. "I thought it would help to have some actual *work* to do here, but I couldn't convince her. I couldn't even get her to argue with me. She was just calm. And quiet. And tired. It was like trying to wrestle a wraith. I wish she'd fight. I'd rather fight."

"What's a wraith?" Jasper asked softly.

"Something made out of smoke," she said. "Sort of. You can see little ones fly away from a candle when it goes out." She took a breath, rallied, and pulled her sense of purpose back together. "Salt. We still need salt."

7

THE TWO MOVED QUICKLY THROUGH THE TACKY
Tavern. Rosa stuffed her pockets full of salt packets.
Jasper put another handful into the pouch he carried.
His clothes had no pockets. Sir Dad was a purist when
it came to anachronistic pockets, which didn't show up
in European clothes until the seventeenth century, so
Jasper had to carry a pouch.

It felt like theft to take so much salt, especially without buying a turkey leg first, but neither one of them
was hungry. Besides, Jasper had already eaten three or
four lifetimes worth of tasteless turkey legs in his years
as a squire and festival kid. He would need to be very,
very hungry to want another one.

Next they ran to Odds Bodkin's Knickknackery Shoppe for a pocketknife and a cigarette lighter. The folding knife had a polished wooden hilt to make it look fancier than it really was. The lighter was a chrome Zippo with sea chantey lyrics etched into the side. Jasper couldn't find anything cheaper. They didn't have enough cash between them. So Jasper held up the items, made eye contact with Mr. Bodkin behind the counter, and tried to communicate urgency.

Mr. Bodkin gave him a skeptical look. Festival performers got *discounts* at the shops and stalls, but they didn't get things for free, and Mr. Bodkin probably wouldn't sell cigarette lighters to eleven-year-olds, anyway.

Jasper didn't want to explain. He wasn't sure where to start. He wasn't sure Mr. Bodkin would remember what he told him if he did try to explain. But he must have looked urgent and serious enough, because Mr. Bodkin nodded and turned his attention back to paying customers. Jasper left the shop with knife, Zippo, and lighter fluid.

"How's this?" he asked. "I'm not sure where to find matches instead. And Nell makes the best knives around here, but she'd never let us use one."

"Should be fine," Rosa said. She filled up the Zippo and tried to light it, but couldn't get it to work.

Sparks shot away from the flint and gears, but the wick wouldn't catch. She kept trying.

"You can keep creepy things out of the festival with this stuff?" he asked.

Rosa hesitated. "Maybe? I think so. But I don't even know what we're dealing with. Or what it's trying to do. Or redo. Or undo." She looked like she wanted to burn something. Her fingertips attacked the lighter. Spark, spark, spark.

"Your mom said you could handle this," Jasper reminded her.

"Yeah." Rosa shut the stubborn Zippo and stuffed it in her pocket. She clearly didn't want to discuss her mother. "Let's go. We should start with the lagoon."

"I can't," Jasper said. "Not yet, anyway. I'll meet you there in a bit."

"Belly dancing?"

"Belly dancing. I have to pass the hat. They don't get paid much without tips."

"Okay. Meet you back at the lagoon."

Jasper turned, ran, and jumped over Handisher, surprised that the tortoise was in his way.

Rosa walked. She tried to move with singular purpose. She did not ask for anyone's permission on her way back to the closed lagoon. She did not acknowledge the guards at the entrance until they crossed their spears and blocked her way.

"Wait just a sec," said one guard, uncomfortable and out of character.

"The lagoon is closed for the day," the other guard said. "We've heard complaints of wild creatures in the forest. Best keep to the larger crowds."

"It was a ghost," Rosa told them. "I was there. And I'm the appeasement specialist." *I'm really just the specialist's daughter,* she thought, but didn't say.

"Ingot isn't haunted," the guards said in unison.

One of them wore a motley uniform of different colors stitched together. The sleeves of his doublet were poufy and cut into long, slashed strips of fancy fabric.

"You're dressed up as a Landsknecht," Rosa noticed. "German mercenary."

"How do you know that?" he asked, incredulous.

Rosa ignored the question. She had little patience for grown-ups surprised by young knowledge. "Landsknechts wore patched finery cut from the corpses of nobles that they killed in battle. Those clothes were *seriously* haunted. That was part of the appeal. Their outfits screamed in pain and rage. They thought it made them more badass. If you want to be really authentic, you should carry hidden speakers and play recordings of horrible yelling wherever you go."

"I tried that already," the guard admitted. "Didn't have the right effect. And no one else understood. I kept having to explain."

"I'm glad you tried," Rosa said. "And now you know that I know about hauntings. So trust me when I tell you that there is one, and that I need to see to it— even though we're in Ingot."

The guards looked uncomfortable and uncertain, but they uncrossed spears and moved out of her way.

Rosa followed the path around the hedge, over the bridge, and up to the lagoon. She took another look at the loop of copper wire and the lurid green mark where the haunted beast had touched it.

8

JASPER WALKED UP AND DOWN THE AISLES BELOW the Mousetrap Stage. He carried a broad-brimmed leather hat and aimed it at appreciative-looking audience members. The hat gradually filled up with coins and small bills, becoming heavy in a satisfying way.

He did all of this without paying attention to any of it.

New possibilities haunted him.

Jasper had never left town, never lived or traveled through anywhere but Ingot. He didn't have out-of-town relatives to visit, and his summer vacations were always locked in orbit around the Renaissance Festival.

Classmates and cousins who did spend summers

elsewhere would come home with ghost stories. They would talk about pebbles piled up at the base of bathroom mirrors, extra place mats at family tables, and candles kept carefully lit at all times. Jasper looked forward to ghost stories in September—even the little fragments of stories, the anecdotes that went nowhere and boiled down to a single, mystified, unsatisfied moment: "Something weird happened and I don't know why!"

No one had ever started the school year with a *local* ghost story.

The show ended. Jasper delivered his hat full of cash to Denise, the lead dancer who also worked the popcorn machine at the second-run theater on Saturdays. Then he ran to the huge prop cabinet behind the pavilion. It was locked, but Jasper was squire to Sir Dad. He had a key.

Jasper opened the cabinet and considered the selection of battered prop weaponry.

A jousting lance would be nice. Or a glaive. Or a boar-sticking spear. Something he could use to keep haunted beasts at bay. But pole-arms for grown-ups—especially grown-ups on horseback—were awkwardly large. And these were all props meant for pretend-fighting. No one carried pointy, dangerous things among the festival crowds. No one used sharp weapons in mock duels or jousts.

Nell made functional things—authentic, museum-quality replicas, entirely unlike the ornate, spiky, goofy fantasy daggers sold by Mr. Smoot of the Unfortunate Sideburns at the other end of the fairgrounds. Nell and Mr. Smoot did not like each other very much. Nell got along with Jasper well enough, but she would never let him borrow something sharp and pointy.

Maybe he didn't need anything sharp or pointy. He grabbed a quarterstaff, which was just a long piece of wood with a leather grip wrapped around the middle. Easy enough to use it as an inconspicuous walking stick. But it might also insist on some distance between himself and dangerous things.

Jasper locked the cabinet, hurried back to the lagoon, argued with the mystified and uncomfortable guards at the entrance, implied that he was there at the specific behest of his mother the queen, and hurried down the path.

Rosa was there, trying to straighten out a tangled length of wire and having a difficult time of it. She dropped the tangle and watched it suspiciously.

"Problem?" Jasper asked.

"I can't decide how to use this stuff," Rosa told him. "I'm not even sure that I *should* use it."

"The dead thing didn't like touching it."

"I know," she said. "But there isn't nearly enough

wire to make a full circle around the whole festival. So I figured we could just stretch it between a couple of trees here. Might help discourage the beastie from coming back this way. It won't work as well as an unbroken circle, but it still might help."

She continued to stare at the wire.

"But?" Jasper prompted.

"But I don't like using metal as a barrier," she said.

"Even if it works?"

"*Especially* if it works."

"Ah," Jasper said, and waited for this to make sense.

Rosa fidgeted with the Zippo. She didn't even try to light it; she just snapped the chrome lid open and shut with one hand.

"Circles aren't supposed to last," she said. "We make them out of chalk, or charcoal, or salt, or scattered bits of paper. We draw lines in the sand. They're signs of respect, and demands for respect. But they aren't stone walls or barbed-wire fences. A circle isn't supposed to say, 'Get out and stay out.'"

"This is a pretty flimsy-looking piece of wire," Jasper pointed out. "It's not a barbed-wire fence."

"It's one step closer to a fence. I still don't like it." She stopped fiddling with the Zippo. "But let's use it anyway. We need time to sort out what's haunting what, exactly, before we can respond. And the haunting thingie might be dangerous. Probably is. To mountain lions, anyway. So a fence might not be the absolute worst idea as long as it's temporary. Can you help me untangle this stuff?"

They strung the wire between trunks and branches like filaments of spider web, until it ran out.

Rosa clapped her hands together. "Now we sharpen two sticks, burn the tips, and use them to draw a great big circle around the whole festival. Then we'll sprinkle salt over the line and hope really hard that it will make any difference. Maybe it won't. To do this right and properly I'd need to find the exact center of the festival and draw a perfect circle around that point. Which I could totally do with a good map and a compass." She picked up a Y-shaped stick, stuck one branching end into the ground, and used the other to draw a perfect circle. But the dirt was hard-packed and didn't really notice the geometry she made. "Or else we could use a really long piece of rope to mark out equal points from the center and then connect those dots. But there are too many people here. They'd trip over the rope. So we'll just make a big, squiggly line around the border of this place instead, like something drawn freehand by a three-year-old."

She broke the stick into two pieces, took out the pocketknife, and attacked one of them like it had said unkind things about her ancestry.

"Have you ever gone exploring in these woods?" she asked while she whittled.

"No," Jasper said. He said it quickly.

"Never? No hiking, or camping, or whatever people do?"

"No," Jasper said. "No one does. Not up there."

Rosa looked at him. She looked right through him. "Why not?"

Jasper shrugged an uncomfortable, defensive shrug. "Couldn't tell you." He badly wanted to change the subject. He wasn't sure why. He wasn't even sure that he wanted to know why.

"Okay," she said. "Never mind." Her voice sounded soothing, which made Jasper suspicious.

She tried to make fire, gave up, and handed him the Zippo. He got it to light. She stuck the sharpened sticks into the small flame.

"There," she said. "Let's draw a messy circle."

9

ROSA AND JASPER MADE A MESSY CIRCLE. THEY gouged it into dirt, leaves, and grass. They drew it in charcoal over stones and tree stumps. They cut through the line of people waiting to buy admission tickets at the front gates. Everyone gave them funny looks, but no one asked for an explanation, and neither Rosa nor Jasper bothered to offer one. They circumnavigated the whole fairgrounds, sprinkled salt packets over the line as they drew it, and finally came back around to where they started.

Rosa kept watching the woods. She had never seen forest before. Trees were isolated things in her city-based experience. They lived out their lives as urban sidewalk decorations, subsisting on soot-soaked rain and canine pee. This made them unhappy. Unhappy trees lead to unhappy library books. All books are former trees, their pages pulped and flattened wood. So librarian appeasement specialists always tend to nearby trees. Rosa used to walk around her old block twice daily to offer clean water.

The trees surrounding Ingot were different. They were not isolated. All together they made a forest, one that covered the faces of mountains and hills on all sides. Rosa couldn't read those faces. She wondered what mountains, hills, and forests might be thinking, and whether or not they noticed the town. She wondered what they remembered. She wondered how much Ingot had forgotten.

"I guess we're done," Rosa said. "We've set the festival apart. That should help. Some. But we need to know more. I wish we knew more."

And I wish Mom were here, she thought. Mom knew how to fit the right action to the right moment, like a book shelved in precisely the right place—or at least she used to be able to, before Rosa's dad got himself killed in such a stupidly shameful way.

Rosa scooped up a couple of old coins from the abandoned jewelry stall. She tossed them into the lagoon, along with her wishes, for absent mermaids to eat.

Then she fished them out of the water again.

Each coin had a square hole in the center, surrounded by Chinese characters. They were made out of copper.

"Let me see that big walking stick," Rosa said.

Jasper handed over his quarterstaff. Rosa dug around in the jewelry stall until she found tacks and a small hammer. She nailed coins to the ends of the staff, driving tacks through square holes.

"Will that help?" Jasper asked.

"Yes," she said. "Maybe. I don't know. But I think so."

"Because the coins are circles?"

"Because they're copper." She handed it back.

"Do all ghosts hate copper?" he asked.

"No," she said. "Most are skittish about some substance in particular. Like salt. Usually salt. But it varies from place to place and haint to haint. This particular ghost doesn't like copper. Not sure why. Wish I knew."

I wish, I wish, I wish.

Jasper struck the ground once with a coin-tipped tap. "I should get back to the stables," he said. "Sir Dad's horse needs a quick grooming and a warmup trot before the joust. And you should come watch! It's fun. Even though it's silly, and based on weird little echoes of history that happened really far away from here. Still fun. Dad loves it. His enthusiasm can fill up the whole field."

"Is the good Sir Morien scripted to win the day, or lose it?" Rosa asked.

Jasper shifted his posture as he slipped into character. "This part of the show is unscripted, and will unfold according to fate and the skill of each knight. Come see for yourself. We should hasten before rabble and groundlings fill up the front row."

"Lead the way," Rosa said.

Jasper led the way. "Dad usually wins," he added.

10

THE JOUST BEGAN WITH TRUMPETED FANFARE, scripted taunts, and genuinely impressive feats of fancy horsemanship. Mounted knights galloped back and forth in front of the queen's pavilion. They speared apples and rings held up by squires. Her Majesty sat in finery and politely applauded. She waved at Jasper. Jasper waved back. *Hi Mom.* Then he juggled a set of five rings for Sir Dad's fancy, climactic feat before the real jousting began.

Sir Morien took his place at the far end of the field. He rode Fiore, a seventeen-hand gray Percheron and his favorite. They would come galloping down and spear all five rings in a single pass—provided that Jasper tossed them up into a single line. This was a new trick, one that they had never performed in public before, but they had it down cold in rehearsal.

Jasper slipped and almost dropped a ring.

It mattered that Rosa was here, in the audience, watching. Weird. This was an unfamiliar sort of feeling. Jasper never thought of himself as theatrical. He didn't like spotlights or standing onstage. He didn't like school presentations at the front of the classroom. He didn't enjoy bluster or posturing. He didn't like to put on a show. That was Sir Dad's thing. Jasper was backup. The assistant. The assist. *Don't look at me. Watch my father in all his glory while he thunders across the field.*

But he still wanted Rosa to notice how well he juggled. And he also didn't, because juggling rings seemed suddenly trivial. Rosa had a much more interesting set of skills. Jasper didn't know how to handle moving statues and bodiless bird wings.

Focus, he thought. *Right now the only thing you need to know how to do is juggle.*

Sir Morien spurred his steed into a gallop. He stood up in the stirrups and steadied himself.

A strong wind came galloping down from the mountains in that same moment.

Rosa felt the temperature suddenly drop. She also felt her sense of time fracture and fragment into isolated moments. Clouds darkened the sky and peered down as if interested in the outcome of the tournament.

She knew what sorts of things could make time stutter alongside sudden gusts of cold air.

Something big, she thought. *That squiggly circle we drew isn't going to help. I should have—*

A broken tree burst through the fairgrounds and knocked over half the pavilion before Rosa could finish the thought.

The tree had flipped itself upside-down. It ran on thick branches that pretended to be legs. Leaves covered the lower half like a long, green gown. Inside that gown the branches snapped and broke, unjointed, unable to bend but bending anyway. Shattered wood scraped against itself as it splintered into knees.

You remember a time when you had knees, Rosa noted, *but you've put on new clothes that don't fit.*

Mud-soaked roots reached up to the sky, and in their center roared the head of a mountain lion. Light burned red inside its gaping mouth.

Oh, Rosa thought. *That's where the head ended up.*

The haunted thing screamed through its stolen head. The crowd scattered, but not very quickly. Crowds do not move fast.

Royal spectators scrambled away from the ruined

pavilion, Jasper's mother among them. She seemed to be limping.

Sir Dad and another knight—Sir Agravain, who owned the local hardware store—tried to hold their ground against the angry tree. But Agravain had never won a joust. He usually tumbled off his horse with excellent comedic timing. His slapstick horsemanship wasn't up to this sort of challenge, so his steed decided to bolt in a sensible panic instead. Sir Agravain fell off and rolled aside—which was what he was best at doing anyway.

Sir Dad kept Fiore from panicking, probably by singing to her. His voice could convince horses to trot calmly through a burning barn.

He called out a challenge, still in character and also very much himself. He was trying to defend the realm, and to distract a dangerous thing before it trampled people beneath all of those branches that it used for legs. Sir Dad charged, raised his lance (the pointy kind, meant to spear apples and juggling rings, and not the blunt kind used for whacking against another knight's shield), and stabbed the tree beast in the center of its trunk.

The lance broke. The haunted thing did not seem to notice or care. It ignored both knights as it lurched across the field.

Jasper didn't have his quarterstaff readily at hand.

But he did have five juggling rings, and realized that they might be more useful, so he tossed them into the tree beast's charging path.

It stumbled and slowed to avoid stepping inside those small circles, but it did not stop.

The crowd scattered like a flock of startled pigeons. A tree with the head of a lion bore down on them, and they got out of the way.

Rosa did not get out of the way.

She dropped to a crouch, clicked the pocketknife open, and gouged a deep ring in the dirt around her. The knife blade broke just as she finished drawing her protective geometry. She tossed the hilt aside and stayed put, perfectly still, while the tree thundered in her direction.

It stopped outside the circle.

Wood creaked, shrieked, and shattered as it bent down. Roots writhed like grasping worms, but they all remained outside the boundary. The open mouth of the mountain lion shone its red lantern glow into Rosa's face.

"Speak to me," she said.

The lion's mouth screamed.

Rosa winced. She looked down and away. A single strand of copper wire caught her attention. It lay

embedded in the bark of a leg-branch. Scorched wood smoked around the metal.

Wisps of smoke also curled up from the medallion around Rosa's neck.

The haunted tree stood and moved wide around her circle, branches creaking. Then it lurched and lumbered toward town.

Rosa followed.

11

HORSES RUN WHEN THEY PANIC. SUDDEN, THUNDER-
ous, directionless freakouts have always helped them
avoid predators. The festival horses indulged in this
instinct just as soon as they saw an otherworldly combi-
nation of predatory animal and upside-down tree—all
of them but Fiore, Sir Dad's own steed, and probably
because Dad sang to Fiore.

The haunted tree did not seem interested in chasing
horses. It lurched away from the fairgrounds. But the
horses did not notice this. They ran, and ran smack into
things like food stalls and fences.

Jasper spotted Jerónimo in the mess and chaos. The
young Belgian horse was already prone to unpredict-

able footwork and sudden lunges, even when he wasn't spooked by a moving tree. Now he tried to outrun his own uprooted hitching post. The post trailed behind him and whacked into his legs, which spurred Jerónimo to further frenzy. He screamed as he ran.

Jerónimo was Jasper's own horse. Sort of. He was Jasper's responsibility, the one he groomed daily. And now he was screaming.

Jasper ran. He tried to catch up with his horse. But Englebert the stable boy got there first.

Oh no, Jasper thought. *Not him.* The older boy had worked at the farm and festival for two summers, just to pay for riding lessons, but he remained willfully inept. Now he had Jerónimo cornered behind Mousetrap Stage.

Englebert tried to calm the horse by yelling at him to be calm. It didn't work. Obviously. Jerónimo jumped sideways and back again, ears flat and tail clamped. He rolled his eyes as though sarcastically panicked.

Jasper slowed down and approached from the side.

Englebert took off his tunic. He clearly intended to lunge at the horse's face and use the cloth as a blindfold. It didn't work. Obviously. Jerónimo shied and reared back as though frightened by a snake underfoot. Then he lunged. The hitching post whipped around like a mace on a chain.

Jasper caught the post before it whacked into him. He only noticed this after he had already caught it. Once he did notice, he pulled. Jerónimo veered away sideways instead of trampling Englebert, and Jasper felt triumphant for one tiny moment before he got pulled off his feet.

The worn tether broke away from the hitching post. Jerónimo galloped off, finally free of the thing that had harried and tormented him. He disappeared into the forest.

Jasper stood up. He knew that he needed to follow his lost horse into the trees. Now. Right now. But he also knew that he wouldn't.

Englebert seemed similarly unwilling to keep up the chase. They picked their way slowly back to the wreckage of the pavilion. Jasper noticed that he still held the hitching post, and dropped it.

He spotted his parents, upright and in charge of things. Then he looked for Rosa, and couldn't find her—but he did find a broken knife and a circle carved in the dirt.

Branches and scattered leaves made a trail away from that spot and through a wrecked hole in the festival wall.

Rosa followed the tree through the festival parking lot. It climbed over cars and crushed them underneath its bulk. Square fragments of windshield glass crunched under Rosa's sneakers as she ran after it.

The tree moved with difficulty. Branches broke away with every step. It made moaning creaks and the sharp snaps of bending, breaking, living wood that wouldn't be alive for very much longer. But it still took long strides. It moved faster than Rosa.

The patron medallion of Catalina de Erauso grew painfully cold. Rosa pulled it out and clutched it in one hand. She tried to remember what she would need to do when she finally caught up to the tree.

Establish a circle around each harmful thing, de Erauso wrote four hundred years ago in *Dialogues of the Skill*, her great book of appeasement. *Nothing is stronger than a circle, nothing more whole in itself, nothing freer in its motion, for the scholars say that motion is most perfect when it rotates around a central point. Draw flawless geometry around the point of danger. Draw flawless geometry around yourself. Understand this boundary between danger and yourself. Understand yourself as dangerous.*

Catalina de Erauso had dressed as a boy and fought as a mercenary in Spain and South America before she became a traveling librarian. She had also dueled and killed at least a dozen people—including her brother, though she didn't know who he was at the time. He haunted her. She taught herself appeasement.

The circle is not a cage. It is not a trap. It is an expression of respect. It is the orbiting danger of each powerful thing within the boundary of its reach.

Rosa wondered what she could use to make a circle. She still didn't have chalk, and her pockets were all out of salt.

She stumbled over a fallen branch, but caught herself before she fell. Then she ran faster. Her legs hurt.

Speak to danger in its language, or offer it your own. The spirits of the living and the spirits of the dead will strive to speak their histories. A librarian must listen.

The tree wouldn't talk to me! Rosa argued back. *Already tried. I'll have to try harder. But first I need it to hold still.*

The trail of broken branches led to the front steps of the Ingot Public Library.

Rosa came to a stumbling, stuttering stop. Her breath seemed to keep going without her. She tried to catch it.

Mom stood at the top of the steps, eye to eye with the head of a lion.

Athena Díaz, the appeasement specialist, threw down two handfuls of shredded paper cut from old encyclopedias—out of date, and out of print, but still soaked with the knowledge of ten thousand things.

The paper scattered like confetti at a wedding. It formed perfect circles when it fell across the library steps; one around the upside-down tree and its skirt of leaves, one around Rosa's mother—which touched the first and formed a figure eight—and one huge, third circle encompassing them both. The final shape looked like an eye with two pupils.

"Hello," Mom said. "I didn't expect this. Thought I'd have more of a break than a single day."

The beast screamed with the lion's mouth. Reddish light glowed brighter inside it.

"Speak," Mom said, resigned. "Find your voice. If you have none left then you may borrow mine." She held out her hand through the place where two circles touched, and took hold of a twisting, muddy root.

"I am no dog you can command to bark," the thing said with her borrowed voice, but so distorted by the mountain lion's mouth that it didn't sound like her.

"Clearly," Mom answered. "You're a cat stuck to a plant. Say what you came here to say. Tell me how you came to be the only haunting in Ingot."

"I am not the only one," the lion's mouth growled. "Give him to me."

Who? Rosa thought.

"Who?" Mom said.

The tree cracked and tore as it leaned forward. "Give him to me. He is already mine, and I know where he hides. I will find him. I will bring remembrance."

"I'm also a servant of memory," Mom said, her voice unshaken when she used it herself.

One of the tree's branching legs caught fire and burned in lurid, shimmering green. "Everyone and every thing within this town and valley will burn in memoriam."

"That sounds less appealing," Mom said.

The green flame spread from the tree to the geometry of paper scraps that surrounded them both. "It will burn."

"No." Mom's voice was not flammable.

"You will not prevent this."

"No," she said again.

"The boundary is breaking. He cannot maintain it. I have come home to claim him."

"No."

"You live in my house!" the thing raged. "You crawl through my cellar!"

This is getting ugly, Rosa thought. She tried to rush into the circle, but the fire grew and kept her out.

"I live here now," Mom said.

"You are unwelcome," said the thing. "This house

is mine, as he is mine, as your voice is now mine. I will take the voice and keep it."

Mom tried to pull her hand away, but the tree root wrapped itself tight around her arm.

Rosa shouted something. She wasn't sure what.

Her mother reached out with her free hand, grabbed the lion's head by its teeth, and tore it away.

The head made a thick, wet sound when it hit the sidewalk. The tree collapsed, still burning. A howling noise faded away southward.

Rosa couldn't see her mother through the wreckage and flame.

12

JASPER FOUND ROSA KNEELING BESIDE A TOWERING bonfire on the library steps. He thought she was tugging on a branch, trying to pull it away from the rest of the blaze. But it wasn't a branch. It was a woman—her mother—who did not budge. Jasper helped pull.

The mountain lion head lay nearby, looking up. Its eyes moved wildly. Its mouth opened and closed twice. Then eyes and mouth stopped moving.

Fire climbed up high and threw sparks in crackling bursts. Rosa yelled her frustration. It sounded like the sort of noise that mountain lions make.

Her mother stirred. She unwound the root that held her arm. Rosa and Jasper half-carried her up the front steps.

A fire truck arrived behind them and doused the burning tree. The blaze billowed steam. It took its time extinguishing. Once gone it left behind a scorched, cracked shape that looked more like bones than branches.

The trio turned away and went inside. They found a big leather chair beside a magazine rack. The chair was fancy, but also old, worn, and patched together with duct tape. Athena settled in and sighed.

"Are you okay?" Rosa asked. "Mom? Tell me you're okay."

Her mom tried to answer. She couldn't.

"Write me a note," Rosa grabbed a Sharpie and a scrap of paper from the suggestion box near the entrance—a wooden box with a slot in the top, through which library patrons could make secret requests, complaints, and invocations.

Mom tried to write. It came out all confused and squiggly.

"What's wrong?" Jasper asked. "Did she hit her head?"

"She lost her voice," Rosa said. Her own voice sounded a thousand miles distant. "A ghost took it. Not just the part she shapes by breathing. All of it."

Mrs. Jillynip came fretting in their direction. "What is going on here? And what is going on *outside*?"

"Shush," Rosa said automatically. Mrs. Jillynip spoke too loudly for a library—even this library, where loud noises would not wake the books or anything asleep between the books.

"Do not shush me, child," snapped the irate librarian. "Who is this?"

Rosa took a breath. Then she took another. "This is your colleague, Ms. Athena Díaz, the best librarian of appeasement you'll ever find anywhere. And she just saved this library from a vengeful tree. Her arm looks banged up. Do you have a first aid kit? One with burn cream? I would use ours, but we haven't unpacked yet so I don't know where it is."

Mrs. Jillynip raised one eyebrow like an axe, but she went back to the front desk and rummaged around for a first aid kit.

Mom closed her eyes. Rosa poked her knee, hard. "Stay awake! Just in case you really did whack your head."

"Are *you* okay?" Jasper whispered.

"Yep," Rosa said quickly. "Fine. Unhurt. No problem. Definitely fine. Yes."

Her voice sounded brittle. He wasn't convinced. "You seem a little twitchy."

"I'm *fine*," she insisted in a very loud whisper. "And Mom is fine. She's going to be fine. You should have seen her. You should have *seen* her! She stood up to the tree. She threw down circles. She was *herself.*"

Rosa wanted to explain what that meant. She wanted Jasper to know just how much respect Mom once commanded among the living and the dead. Because she was the best. Vengeful spirits set aside centuries-old grudges to chat with her. Lost and over-due books came home when she called. Even the most malicious, gossip-mongering, disembodied spirits of cell phones and pocket screens hushed in her com-pany. And when the Miasmic Thing tried to devour storytime last summer, Athena Díaz sent it limping back down to the boiler room with a bell around its neck. She was the absolute best.

But then Rosa's father died. Shamefully. Because he turned out to be the *worst* appeasement specialist. And Mom waned. The job took more out of her, even the easy bits of the job that Rosa could have handled. So Rosa started to handle them. She dealt with minor hauntings so her mother wouldn't have to. She pro-tected the silent books, dealt with rogue statues, and listened for the Miasmic Thing's tinkling bell while she waited for Mom to return to herself.

It had felt good to be useful, to become a special-ist in her own right. And being useful had helped Rosa distract herself from the absence of her beloved, idiotic dad and his embarrassed smile. "Don't tell your mother," he'd say after blundering through something that should have been easy. And Rosa would promise, delighted to share his secrets. She would help him clean up whatever mess he had made. Because it felt good to be useful.

Rosa wanted to explain all of it to Jasper, but she couldn't speak. For one single moment of panic she thought that her own voice was gone, stolen away by a haunting in an unhaunted place. Then she found her voice, but she still couldn't say much. "Mom should be fine. We just need to find that ghost."

"How do we do that?" Jasper asked.

"I don't know," she said. "But I think I need your help. Maybe. Probably. Please. Unless you're too busy picking up broken pieces of festival tomorrow. I guess our messy circle didn't protect it much."

"I can help," he said quickly, because he did want to help her hunt for haunted things—and also because he felt uncomfortable and wanted to change the subject. So far he had avoided thinking about the broken stalls, or the shredded remains of the royal pavilion, or the trampled fortune-teller's tent where Doris the Seer threw down tarot cards. He wanted something to do instead. Something important. "Find me tomorrow. I'll be at the farm. And I should probably get back there. We have some spooked horses to soothe."

And maybe Jerónimo made it home, he thought. *Maybe he'll be waiting outside the stable. Maybe.*

"Okay," said Rosa. "I'll find you. Don't take off that bracelet. Feel free to wear any other copper you can find. Stick copper coins to yourself with Band-Aids, maybe."

"I'll keep the bracelet on," he promised. "Bye."

"Bye," Rosa said.

Her mother tried to speak, and couldn't. She tried to wave, but the gesture became just a flick of the hand.

Jasper left. The painted eyes of Bartholomew Theosophras Barron did not watch him in the lobby. Outside the sun was setting. Someone had hauled away the ruined tree, leaving a scorched sidewalk behind.

Mrs. Jillynip came fretting back to Rosa with an ancient and battered first aid kit. The Band-Aids inside had probably given up, died away, and lost all their adhesive.

"Thank you," Rosa said. She meant it, though she might not have sounded like she meant it.

The older librarian gave a terse nod. "Tend to your mother," she said. "It is good to meet you, Mrs. Díaz."

"Ms. Díaz," Rosa said automatically, but Mrs. Jillynip didn't seem to notice.

"I'll be closing up the library and leaving now," the older librarian said. "If you must come and go your-selves, then you'd best have your own way to lock up." She handed over two keys to the front door. "I trust you'll keep out of Special Collections while I'm away."

Mrs. Jillynip turned abruptly, switched off most of the lights, and left before Rosa could respond to her mix of condescension and kindness.

"Hi," she said to her Mom.

Mom smiled a little, but it wasn't really a response.

Rosa rolled up her mother's sleeve, cleaned mud from the scrapes and cuts, and applied goopy, greasy burn cream. Then she bandaged up the whole arm, and probably used too many bandages. It looked lumpy.

"Do you know what that was?" Rosa asked. She couldn't help asking. "Do you know what used that tree as a new set of clothes?"

Mom struggled against her lack of voice.

"Never mind," Rosa said quickly. "Never mind. Come on. I'm hungry. Let's unpack some rice and beans in our dungeon apartment."

They went downstairs where all of their familiar things were stacked in silent, unfamiliar piles.

13

JASPER WOKE EARLY. HE USUALLY DID. AND ON THIS morning his brain instantly snapped to fully awake. He had haunted things to think about.

The Chevalier home was a very old farmhouse. Most of it creaked whenever stepped on or leaned against. Jasper knew which floorboards had the loudest voices, but he still couldn't avoid creaking noises entirely while he moved around upstairs. Not that he was trying to be sneaky. Both parents would be up already. He just liked to move without making much noise.

As in most old farmhouses, the bathrooms were tiny and the staircase too narrow for anyone wider than three sheets of paper. Broad-shouldered Dad had to turn himself sideways to go up or down the stairs, but Jasper still fit. In the bathroom he used very pale Band-Aids to stick pennies to each shoulder. In the stairwell he skipped several steps on his way down. He also skipped breakfast until after he had checked in on the stable.

He brought his staff with him. The coin at the tip made a clink, clink, clink noise against the driveway and the stable's cement floor.

Jerónimo was still missing. Twelve stalls on the right stood full, but only eleven on the left.

The four grooms who worked for the family went about their business, performing their morning rituals with brush and sponge, checking the bandages over yesterday's cuts and scrapes. And the horses themselves seemed fine, unhaunted by memories of a haunted tree. Horses spook easily, but they also calm down quickly.

Jasper mucked out Jerónimo's stable and put down fresh bedding, even though he didn't need to, even though the horse hadn't come home last night. Jasper still needed to do this. He did it *every* morning. It meant that the day would unfold as it should.

He went back inside the house. His staff clinked against the driveway as he walked.

The Chevalier kitchen, like the Renaissance Festival itself, was a gleefully anachronistic place. Their shiny chrome fridge sat beside a stone hearth large enough to stand up in. Sometimes they boiled stew in a massive cauldron over an open fire, but not very often. It set off the smoke alarm. And good stew takes forever to make properly.

A long wooden table took up most of the kitchen. It had benches rather than chairs, and seemed suitable for feasting bands of merry warriors.

Mom and Dad—Emily and Morris Chevalier— sat sipping ye olde cappuccinos with the other two directors of the Ingot Renaissance Festival: Timothy Rathaus, who used to joust with Dad at the very beginning but had since retired from the lists to run the Tacky Tavern, and Nell MacMinnigan the smith, who was still the smith. Mr. Rathaus sported a trim goatee on his chin. Nell had short red hair, a torn T-shirt, and an armband that swirled around her smithy-widened bicep. She rarely laughed. Right now she looked very far away from laughing.

Jasper got himself a bowl of cereal, joined the adults at the table, and listened to them talk over and around him.

The four directors met to decide the fate and future of the Ingot Renaissance Festival, large portions of which had been flattened by a tree yesterday. And they seemed to *remember* that tree stampede, which was a huge relief to Jasper. They didn't pretend that it had not happened. But they also didn't seem concerned that it had happened.

"We can reopen tomorrow," Mr. Rathaus insisted. "We can rebuild by then."

"Seems doable," said Mom, cautiously optimistic. "But I might have to cut down on royal processions." She stretched out her leg. Jasper scooted aside to give her sprained and bandaged ankle more room on the bench.

"We really can't afford to close for longer than that," Rathaus went on. "Not so early in the season."

"We also owe it to the out-of-town performers," Dad agreed. "I doubt they've even recouped travel expenses yet."

Nell hunched her shoulders and stared at her mug as though scrying their future in the dregs of cappuccino foam. (Jasper knew and liked her well enough to think of her as Nell rather than Ms. MacMinnigan.)

"A few out-of-towners have skipped already," she said. "They know what can happen to historical reenactments in haunted places. Echoes of actual history crop up to argue with performers."

"Ingot isn't haunted," said Mom, Dad, and Rathaus in unison.

Nell looked up. "Trees don't decide to flip over and run downhill all by themselves."

Rathaus shook his head. "That's just the exception that proves the rule."

"Nope, nope, *nope*," Nell insisted. "The rule is that this *never* happens. Ever. Not here. But it happened anyway. So that exception very definitely *disproves* the rule."

She couldn't convince them. Rathaus only pretended to listen. Mom had her mind firmly set to optimistic problem-solving. Dad was tired, a little sad, and clearly worried about the horses. But he couldn't imagine shutting down the festival. He couldn't see it as necessary, or even possible. And a haunted Ingot was an alien idea to them, one that they couldn't even look at directly.

Jasper had felt much the same way before Rosa made him a rough bracelet out of copper wire.

"We have safety volunteers patrolling up and down the tree line," Rathaus said.

Nell was not mollified. "I saw some of that. Local boys itching to take some kind of action. They formed their own ghost hunting militia. Now they're all marching around in costume with pointy, poorly balanced pole arms they bought or borrowed from Smoot. Young Humphrey, the mayor's own kid, is carting around a homemade flamethrower with brass gears glued on to make it look sort of Victorian. I feel very, very safe now that those brave lads stand ready to protect their homes and kill some ghosts. But you *can't* kill something that's already skipped through dying and come out the other side. We aren't used to hauntings here. We don't know how to respond. I'm pretty sure that this isn't how we should."

"We do have a new appeasement specialist in town," Jasper told them.

Rathaus gave a dismissive chuckle. "But this is *Ingot*," he said. "We've never needed one of those before."

The three directors wouldn't budge. They still remembered what happened, but those events had ceased to be viscerally real or cause for concern. Something had sanded away the rough edges of their memories.

Nell gave up, swallowed the dregs of her cappuccino, and went outside to smoke.

Jasper slurped down his cereal milk and followed. He found her on the porch, stuffing tobacco into a long wooden pipe with the tip of her pinky finger. Then she looked for a light.

He gave her the Zippo.

"What's this?" she asked, suspicious and muttering around her pipe stem. "Are you taking up bad habits? Smoking is all kinds of bad. I've inhaled so many fumes from melting down metal that I figure my lungs are wrecked already, but yours aren't. Not yet. Stand back. Even second-hand stuff is bad."

"No bad habits," Jasper said. "Rosa needed fire yesterday. The appeasement specialist. So we picked this up."

"That the girl I saw you racing around with?"

Jasper nodded.

"Interesting." Nell lit her pipe, puffed the smoke, and looked out across the fields like a sailor watching the sea. "We've got ourselves a tiny specialist."

"Two of them," Jasper said. "One is less tiny. But she's in rough shape after she took down the tree."

"That's unfortunate," Nell said. She gave him back the Zippo. He stuck it in his pocket. "Still. Took down the tree. Good to hear. Your father didn't have much luck jousting against it. Which came as no surprise."

Jasper considered her spiraling piece of jewelry. "Maybe his lance wasn't made of the right metal. Is that copper on your arm?"

"Mostly," Nell said. "Almost entirely. It's bronze, and bronze is just copper with a little bit of tin tossed in for strength and flavor. Is there something I should know about copper?"

He showed her the thin wire bracelet on his own wrist. "The ghost didn't like touching this stuff."

"Is that right, " she said. "I've got a bit of a Bronze Age collection back at the shop. Not much. Collectors usually go for more renaissancy replicas, but I do have a bit . . ." She stopped. "Forget it. Forget I said anything. And don't go telling anyone else about this copper business. The very last thing I need is to have every would-be ghost hunter come begging for my Bronze Age collection. It wouldn't protect them, or anyone else. It would just put danger in their hands—the sort of danger that might lash out at anybody. Know what adrenaline does?"

"Yes," he said in a way that would, hopefully, forestall a lecture about adrenaline. Sir Dad loved to give lengthy explanations of things that Jasper already knew, so he had to endure this pretty often. "It makes you faster. And stronger."

"It also makes your hands shake." Nell took the pipe out of her mouth and pointed the stem at him. "No matter how brave you are, or level-headed, or filled with knightly virtue, your hands will still shake from the force of adrenaline and you will be simply unable to do anything precise with anything pointy. Unless you practice for *years*. And keep practicing. Every day. Our new, volunteer militia of ghost hunters aren't so skilled. Maybe they're trying to be usefully brave, but I figure they'll be clumsily dangerous instead. And I won't add to that disaster. I won't give weapons to boys who want to feel more in control than they really are. Won't make any difference against an undead, irate tree anyway. You just stand clear of dead trees. Can't kill ghosts with a Bronze Age spear."

"Can't kill ghosts at all," Jasper said, by which he meant, *I'm with you. We're on the same page. Stop reading me that page aloud.*

Nell crossed her blacksmithing arms. The left one bulged inside its armlet. "Nice staff," she said, nodding at the spot where it leaned beside the door.

"Thanks."

She peeked at the old coin hammered onto the end. "Zhou Dynasty, looks like. Probably a replica. Can't read the characters. One of my tattoos is in Chinese. Got it when I was young and dumb. It was supposed to be a list of the five elements. Turns out it reads, 'This is a tattoo.'"

"At least that's accurate," Jasper said.

"Yeah," she said. "Could be worse. I wonder what your coins say. I wonder how much it matters. But I'm glad you've got that staff. Proper kind of defensive weapon. You can use it to keep your distance from dangerous things without becoming a flailing, reckless, stabby sort of dangerous thing yourself. I'll worry less about you if you walk softly with that. But don't go around thinking that a stick makes you invincible. It's not a talisman. It's not a symbol of your mightiness. It's just a stick."

Jasper took it by the leather-wrapped grip in the center. He didn't swing it around or do anything flashy, even though he really wanted to.

"Just a stick," he promised.

Nell went to the railing and knocked ashes from her pipe onto the lawn. "Thank your parents for the coffee. I should make my rounds and check all the horseshoes." As a real, actual blacksmith Nell was also the town farrier and horseshoe expert.

"The grooms checked already," Jasper pointed out.

"Yeah, but I don't trust them to do it right. And then I need to go back to the fairgrounds, clean up my smithy, hide my wares from amateur ghost hunters, and get ready to reopen. Which is, for the record, a terrible idea."

"Bye Nell."

She waved and headed for the stables with her pipe in her teeth.

14

ROSA WOKE UP THAT MORNING WITHOUT KNOWING where she was, or what time it was. *Probably the middle of the night*, she figured, given the absolute darkness around her. But she needed the bathroom, so she climbed out of bed—except the bed wasn't a bed so much as a mattress on the floor, and Rosa couldn't find the bathroom because it wasn't where it was supposed to be, and also because piles of boxes stood between her and wherever the bathroom had hidden itself.

She knew where she was, now: in Ingot, underneath the library. But that knowledge didn't help her find the bathroom in the dark.

"Why do we live in a basement?"

Mom switched on a lamp. The sudden change was eye-stabbing. Rosa shut hers, and then blinked them back open.

"Sorry I woke you up," she said. "What time is it? Four in the morning?"

Mom fumbled around for her phone. She looked at it and tried to make sense of it.

Rosa started to get worried. "Can you tell what it says?" She grabbed a book from one of several dozen boxes marked "books" in black Sharpie. "Can you read this?"

Mom took the book. Her forehead furrows deepened as she concentrated.

"You can't," Rosa realized. "I think you understand me. You seem to understand me. But that's my voice. Not yours. And when you read, you hear your own voice in your head. Yours is gone. So the words aren't in your head."

Mom set down the book and smiled a wistful and not-at-all reassuring sort of smile. Rosa tried to swallow the understanding that her mother, a librarian, could no longer read.

"I'll find your voice," she promised. "I'll get it back. I will." She glanced at the phone. "And it's almost *ten o'clock*. But we live in a basement without real windows, so we can't tell the difference between the middle of the night and the middle of the morning. I'm going to start pitching a tent on the main floor."

She navigated the cardboard labyrinth on her way to the bathroom, where she stacked up a cairn of pebbles underneath the mirror. Then she lit a candle stub with a match and set it beside the cairn. Maybe that mattered. Maybe it didn't. Nothing on either side of the mirror seemed to notice or care. Nothing used the candle flame to pass from one side to the other. But she still felt better for doing it. And the bathroom began to smell a little less musty.

"Hi Dad," she said, softly so her mother wouldn't hear.

Breakfast was meager. They found the last of the bagels from their favorite shop in the city, picked up on moving day and kind of stale. They had no butter, cream cheese, or jam, and couldn't find the toaster, so they had to content themselves with chewing dry bagels.

"I'll get groceries later," Rosa promised. "Just as soon as I figure out where the grocery store is."

Mom looked like she wanted to handle such things.

"You can't read the labels. You might come home with squid jerky and prunes."

Mom furrowed her brow again. She looked wounded and dissatisfied.

"Do you know where we packed the tool belts?" Rosa asked, quickly. *You shouldn't need your voice to remember that. And you've always been able to find lost things. Always. Even the books that deliberately mis-shelved themselves couldn't hide from you for long.*

Her mother homed in on a particular pile of boxes, removed the two on top, and ripped packing tape away from a box in the middle. Then she pulled out both belts and handed Rosa her own.

The buckle made a satisfying noise when Rosa clipped it on. The weight felt right and fitting.

"Thanks," she said. "Now I need to do a little research. And go for a hike. But I'll be back soon." She kissed her mother on the cheek. They made eye contact, and held it, but Rosa couldn't tell what that meant—if it meant anything. Mom couldn't seem to make it signify. She didn't have a voice.

"I'll find it," Rosa promised.

Her mother set her own skills to finding the lost and disassembled pieces of their coffee maker.

Rosa filled a travel mug with water. She dumped an obscene amount of salt into the water and stirred up the mix until the salt dissolved. Then she plucked a loose hair from the back of Mom's shirt. Mom didn't notice. Rosa dropped a snipped-off piece of the hair into salty water before waving an unseen good-bye.

She took the borrowed first aid kit upstairs and headed directly for Special Collections. (She left the travel mug on the floor, just outside the doorway, because she knew better than to bring liquid into Special Collections.)

"Good morning, Mrs. Jillynip," Rosa said. "Thank you for this."

"Good morning . . . child," said Mrs. Jillynip, who had not yet asked Rosa's name and now pretended that she didn't need to. "Your mother is well, I hope."

Not really, Rosa thought. "Well enough," she said aloud.

"I am glad to hear it," said Mrs. Jillynip. She took the kit and turned away, clearly expecting the conversation to be over.

"Who hired her, exactly?" Rosa asked.

The other librarian raised her eyebrows like cautious boxing gloves. "Excuse me? We posted notice of the new position here, and your mother applied for the job. It was my understanding that she sought out a quieter life than the one she had previously led."

"That's what I thought, too," Rosa said. "But now I'm thinking that somebody wanted the best appeasement specialist they could find to live in Ingot. Somebody knew to expect ghostly troubles here. Who was it? Do you know?"

Mrs. Jillynip turned her back on the forbidden spiral staircase to avoid glancing in that direction.

Rosa pretended not to notice.

"I really don't know what you mean, child," the other librarian insisted. "Is there something else I can help you with?"

Rosa let the matter of invitations and spiral staircases drop. There *was* one other thing that she needed.

"Yes, please. Thank you for offering. I'd like to go through the map collection."

Mrs. Jillynip hovered like a vengeful hummingbird while Rosa picked through old maps with white-gloved fingers.

The paper made crinkling noises. The older librarian twitched.

"What *precisely* are you looking for?"

"Maps of Ingot," Rosa said.

And the hills around it, she thought without saying. She paged back through time and watched the town shrink all the way down to a few buildings gathered around a single crossroads.

Main Street ran directly east-west between two mountain tunnels. The highway still ran through those tunnels. No one ever traveled *over* the mountains that surrounded Ingot—only underneath them.

Why build a town here at all? Rosa thought. *This place is really hard to get to.*

Isabelle Road crossed Main Street and ran south, away from the tiny center of town and into the surrounding hills. But the road ran out of map and disappeared off the edge of the paper before Rosa could see where it went.

Be wary of absence, Catalina de Erauso wrote. *The empty circle. The silence that bespeaks a missing voice. The place where your opponent's sword has not yet struck.*

Rosa checked the dates. "These are barely a century old. Are they the earliest maps we have?"

Mrs. Jillynip made a disapproving noise, as though Rosa had cast doubts on the map collection—or on the town's age and respectability. "They are."

Rosa took off the little white gloves and gave them back. "Thank you for your help."

"You are welcome, child," Mrs. Jillynip said, clearly unsure what it was she had helped with, and possibly unsure whether or not Rosa was actually welcome.

Rosa hitched up her tool belt, retrieved the travel mug, and headed out. She had work to do. She marched underneath the elaborately mustached portrait of Bartholomew Theosophras Barron in the front lobby. Then she turned around and came back.

Both of the bathroom doors were propped open.

She looked inside the women's room. Someone had removed all the pipes and fixtures. The sinks looked headless. Rosa peered into the men's room. It was a grimier place, as expected. It also stood bereft of plumbing.

Someone had come in the night and confiscated a whole lot of copper.

"Be wary of absence," Rosa said to herself.

She checked the front doors, but the locks and latches were not scratched or otherwise damaged. Nothing had broken into the library from outside.

Rosa went out and sat on the front steps. She took the lid off the mug.

"Find me another missing piece of her," she whispered at the salty water. "Inside, or outside? Something is haunting the library. Something else is haunting the hills above Ingot. Where should I start? Which way should I go?"

The hair spun like a compass needle. The follicle pointed away from the library and into the hills. Rosa looked. She saw a patch of scarlet in the distance. Something had shocked several trees into an early autumn, right about where Rosa had seen a flash of light yesterday. Something had taken a piece of Athena Díaz back to that same spot.

Rosa sealed up her compass-mug and clipped it to her belt. She set off southward, toward the fairground and Chevalier Farm, toward the place where Isabelle Road fell off the edge of the map.

15

THE CHEVALIER FARMHOUSE WAS LARGE AND painted grayish green. Rosa climbed onto the front porch. She whispered a courteous hello to whatever may or may not lurk underneath it. First impressions were always important to household spirits.

Nothing rustled under her feet. Rosa wondered if this household *had* any spirits. Maybe they kept low and silent, because this was Ingot. Maybe they had been driven out. Maybe they had never been here at all. Maybe this house, and this farm, and this whole town had always stood empty of all but the living.

She knocked. A blonde woman opened the door and stood in the doorway. The woman held a coffee mug shaped like a knight's helmet.

"Good morning. My name's Rosa. Is Jasper home?"

"Hello there," the woman said. "I'm Mrs. Chevalier. Jasper's mom."

"Oh," said Rosa. "But you're white."

"True," said Mrs. Chevalier.

"Well noticed!" Jasper's dad called out from somewhere inside the house. "She's observant, that one."

"Good morrow to you, Sir Morien," Rosa called after him.

"And to you, Lady Librarian," he answered back.

"Jasper does look a little more like his father," Mrs. Chevalier said smoothly. "And I think he might be back in the stables. You can look for him there. But try not to shout, or do anything sudden and loud."

"Thanks!" Rosa said, and hurried off the porch. She didn't think she had made the best impression on the Chevalier household.

The stable doors were open. The inside was dimly lit and full of thick, musty smells. Horses shuffled and stamped in their stalls. Rosa didn't know much about horses, or how to listen to horse behaviors. She moved cautiously. These beasts were very much bigger than she was, and she didn't speak their language or understand their rules. A chalk circle would be poor defense against a charging, kicking horse.

Jasper stood in the entrance to one stall. The beige horse beside him suddenly stuck its head in the air and bared its teeth. Jasper looked around. He spotted Rosa, and waved. Then he offered the horse an apple. It reached out carefully with its face, took the apple, and left behind a whole handful of drool in Jasper's open palm. He wiped the drool on the leg of his pants.

"This is Agrippa," Jasper said. "He's been grazing on clover lately. Makes him spit more."

"Hi Agrippa," Rosa said.

The horse looked her over with one large, pale eyeball. Its—his—iris ran sideways, like a tipped-over cat's eye. Rosa found that deeply unsettling. Then Agrippa exhaled a burst of warm air at her face. She flinched.

"That means hi," Jasper explained. "You don't need to worry about Agrippa. He's old, wise, cold-blooded, and doesn't lash out or spook easily."

"Okay," Rosa said. "I thought horses were mammals, though."

"Cold-blooded *temperament*, not biology. He isn't reptilian."

"Okay," Rosa said again. She still regarded the horse as though he might be some sort of dinosaur. "Do your parents spook easily? They're both pretty relaxed after yesterday. Not braced for a whole stampede of haunted trees."

"Yeah," Jasper said. "I noticed that, too. So I dropped some pennies in their shoes and talked my mom into wearing copper jewelry. But I can't really tell if it helped. They remember the tree. But they don't want to. And it's like they're trying to ignore the memory until it goes away."

"Have they always lived here?" Rosa asked. "Both of them?"

"Mostly. They're both from here, anyway. Went away to college and then moved right back. Why?"

"I think this kind of amnesia is habit-forming. They've been forgetting for a long while. Longer than you have. Maybe it's easier for you to remember." Rosa didn't want to dwell too much on parents and their missing pieces. "I *hope* it's easier for you, anyway. Let's test that out. Want to come hiking?"

Of course he wanted to come. Jasper grabbed his quarterstaff and set off, ready to face whatever haunted beasts might prowl around the borders of Ingot. But he balked when Rosa turned left at the end of the driveway and hiked south, up into the foothills.

She kept right on going. He took a breath, pushed himself after her, and hurried to catch up. The coin on his staff clinked against the road. Then pavement gave way to packed dirt and small weeds and the tip made a muffled thunking sound instead.

"Cars don't come through here, I guess," Rosa said. "But *something* does. It isn't completely overgrown. The dirt in the middle is packed down and plant-free. Maybe people still use it on foot. Or bike. Or horseback."

"We don't ride horses up this way," Jasper said quickly.

Rosa looked around. "But it's a nice path through the woods. Good view of the valley behind us. No cars. Seems perfect for riding."

"We don't ride up this way," he said again.

Rosa said nothing, but she said it loudly.

The road narrowed further until only the footpath remained, worn smooth but surrounded by forest. The trees and brush leaned close on either side and scratched at their arms and sleeves.

"You know a fair bit about history, right?" Rosa asked as they hiked on.

"Can't help it," said Jasper. "Both parents walk around wearing history. Medieval Europe is their favorite flavor, but they're also members of the local Historical Society. They read up on all kinds."

"When was Ingot founded?" Rosa asked, her voice casually innocent.

"Why?" Jasper asked, suspicious.

"Do you know?"

"Of course I know: 1899. Founded by Bartholomew Theosophras Barron and his wife, Isabelle."

"Okay," Rosa said. "Now *why* was it founded?"

"That's . . . kind of a dumb question."

"No it isn't," Rosa argued. "Something must have brought people out here. Did they throw darts at a map? Or shoot an arrow into the sky and say, 'Let's go that way and build a town!' This place is pretty inconvenient. Hard to get to. Takes effort. The only way in is a highway punched through mountains. Why did settling people spend all that effort?"

"You don't like it here," Jasper said.

"No. I don't. But that's not why I'm asking."

"Well, feel free to ask my parents about local history when we get back. I'm sure they know."

"I'm sure they don't," Rosa said.

Jasper hit the ground harder with his staff as they hiked.

The trail veered around the banks of a small lake. It looked pretty. But someone had nailed several signs to the trees around it. DO NOT SWIM. DO NOT DRINK. WATER UNSAFE. NO FISHING. NO HUNTING. NO TRESPASSING.

Rosa picked up a pebble and tossed it in.

Jasper flinched when it plunked into the water.

"What happened here?" she wondered aloud.

Jasper shook his head. He didn't know. He didn't want to know. He felt the opposite of curious—an intense and flinching distaste for ever knowing.

Rosa gave him a long look. He looked away first, and felt himself growing angry. He couldn't figure out why he would be. He expected to feel excellent and adventurous about accompanying an appeasement specialist on her ghostly errand. But he didn't.

"You're pissed," she said.

"Yes," he agreed.

"You've been getting grouchier as we go."

"You've been getting more and more rude as we go."

She turned to face him. "What's at the end of this road?"

The question felt like a sharp stick poking at his face. "What?"

"This road," Rosa pressed. "You live on it. The center of town is *that* way. What's *this* way?"

"I don't know," he said. "Nothing is."

"Then the trail wouldn't be here. The road would just stop at the farm and fairgrounds. Why is it here? Where is it going?"

"I don't know."

"Why not? You should."

"I didn't think this hike included a quiz."

Rosa crossed her arms and cocked her head sideways. "You're getting seriously angry."

"You're *always* angry!" His own voice surprised him. Jasper didn't shout much.

"True," she said. "I like to feel angry about things that need fixing. Helps me try to fix them. I like to burn that feeling as fuel. But this seems to be burning you instead. And I'm pretty sure that your mom, your dad, old Mrs. Squillypip, and the full membership of the Ingot Historical Society have no idea where this road goes, either."

Jasper stood and seethed.

She dropped her voice. "I also think this anger isn't entirely yours. Some of it might be. But some of it's borrowed."

The seething lessened, just a little, as soon as she said that.

"I can feel it," she went on. "Not as strong as you do, I'm guessing, since I'm not local. But I can still feel it. And it definitely isn't mine. I've got plenty. I know what it tastes like. I can tell the difference. This is coming from somewhere else. And it's making your bracelet send off little wisps of smoke."

Jasper considered his smoky bracelet. It felt cold around his wrist. So did the two pennies stuck to his shoulders with Band-Aids.

He tried to figure out whether any of the anger he felt was his own, and decided that some of it was. "Quit being such a snob about my hometown."

"Okay," she said cheerfully, and started hiking again. "Teach me that sea chantey. The one on the Zippo. If it's good for hoisting sail, it should be good for hiking."

Jasper taught her the chorus.

Away, haul away, we'll heave and hang together,
Away, haul away, we'll haul away soon.
Away, haul away, we're bound for bitter weather.
Away, haul away, we'll haul away soon.

"Is the whole song like that?" Rosa asked. "'Something bad's about to happen and we probably deserve it?'"

"That's *every* sea chantey," Jasper said. "Something bad is always about to happen to sailors. Might as well sing through it."

16

THEY SANG UNTIL THE TEMPERATURE DROPPED
around them. The sunlight weakened above them. The
forest thinned beside them. They walked on in silence,
and they walked more slowly.

"The leaves are red," Jasper noticed. "They're
dying. Like this is October instead of midsummer."

"Maybe it is," Rosa said. "Here, anyway."

Jasper tripped over something, and shouted.

"Shhhh," Rosa said.

"Don't shush me, librarian," Jasper shot back. He
wanted to shout again. He held his breath instead. That
didn't really work. The breath came sputtering out. He
expected Rosa to laugh at the noise, but she didn't.

"You've made it this far," she said. "All the way to the red trees. We're close." She uncapped her travel mug and checked the compass. "You can do this. You can make it to the top of this trail. Call me names if you want, but try not to shout."

She kicked at the dirt to see what he had tripped over. "It's a rail. A rusty iron rail, like a train track."

"Pretty sure we've never had a train up here in the mountains," Jasper said.

She went on. He grumbled and followed. They hiked up over one more rise, and then stopped. They had no choice but to stop.

The trail ended in a wall of rolling, roiling mist.

It looked like a glass wall with a cloudy, foggy day on the other side—but without glass. The wall was simply a line the mist could not cross, and that line was made of copper.

All sorts of oddments had been fused, riveted, and hammered together on the forest floor: wires and pipes, teakettles and pots, small statues and lumps of slag that used to be pennies. Most of it was old and stained darkly green. But one part of the copper boundary was made out of newer, shinier stuff. It looked freshly hammered into place. Rosa recognized sink fixtures from the library bathroom.

"This must stretch across the whole valley," she

said. "One long, unbroken copper ring around Ingot. It's huge. I've never even heard about a circle this huge." She knelt for a closer look.

Letters had been etched into a flattened length of pipe—one word, repeated over and over again.

Λήθη Λήθη Λήθη Λήθη Λήθη Λήθη Λήθη

"Anon?" Jasper wondered. "It means soon. 'I'll see you anon.'"

Rosa shook her head. "Greek letters. It says 'lethe.' Forgetting. Banishment." She spit out the word like she couldn't get it away from her mouth fast enough. "It means somebody did this. On purpose. Someone banished all the ghosts from Ingot *on purpose*."

"Now *you're* pissed," Jasper said. "I thought you were used to anger."

"Not this much of it." Her voice was an icicle held like a knife. "Banishment is awful. It always backfires. Always. Even if you think you're doing it for good reasons. And the ghosts don't go very far. I think they're still here. All of them." She stood up, faced the wall, and threw her voice at it. "Aletheia."

Mist rolled back and away from that word.

Figures crowded together where the mist had been.

They had made themselves out of leaves and twigs, clumps of dirt and coiling vines, piles of stones and falling branches. Some stood three times as tall as Rosa or

Jasper. Others stood barely taller than the line of copper that kept them away. They watched the children through makeshift faces.

One figure crouched down close, directly across the copper line. She had dust-made features and a gown of scarlet leaves. The gown billowed around her. She poked and prodded at the metal with a hand made of twigs, and then flinched away from a flash of green light.

"Talk to me," Rosa said. "Please. You took something from my mother. She needs it back."

The ghost smiled. Her teeth were small stones.

"I am enjoying this voice," she used it to say. The voice sounded faint, as though a thick glass window stood between them. "Your dear mother may call upon me herself after the circle breaks. We will all haunt this valley together then. I may be persuaded to share."

Rosa pleaded, though she tried not to. "There must be something I can do, or trade."

The ghost provoked another green flash. "There is nothing."

"What about *him*?" Rosa asked.

"You're not talking about me, are you?" Jasper whispered.

"No, of course I'm not talking about you," Rosa whispered back. "But yesterday, when she was a tree, she came to the library looking for some sort of him."

The ghost put both hands on the copper barrier. She did not flinch this time. Red leaves began to burn. The figure collapsed, and then remade herself with ashes.

"He is here," she said, the stones of her smile dark with soot.

Mist rolled back and covered the figures again. It stopped short at the copper barrier.

Jasper heard a low growling noise.

Rosa didn't seem to notice. She stared at the swirling mist and looked like she might try to jump right through.

The noise grew louder.

"Rosa? Something's coming."

She just stood and muttered to herself. "A little bit of banishment brought down a whole library branch, back in the city. I saw it happen. And that was just one banished poltergeist. This copper circle is *huge*. It's been here for a hundred years. It's got thousands of ghosts gathered around it, pushing against it, trying to come home. The backlash is going to be so much worse."

Jasper recognized the growling noise as an engine. "Come on, librarian!" He grabbed Rosa's arm and pulled her back into the trees.

An old, rust-covered motorcycle came riding across the mountainside, parallel to the copper barrier.

It stopped and puttered where Jasper and Rosa had stood just a few heartbeats ago. Various tools, a blow-torch, and random pieces of copper filled up a sidecar.

The driver dismounted, unfolding lanky arms and legs. He wore large goggles and a long mustache. He looked like a pilot from the very first age of airplanes.

He also looked like the lobby portrait of Bartholomew Theosophras Barron, founder of Ingot.

Barron kicked at the barrier, testing his new patch of shiny metal. The wall above it took on the deep green-ish gray of thunderclouds. He nodded, satisfied. Then he climbed onto his bike and took Isabelle Road down the mountain.

Rosa glared at the valley and the direction the bike had gone. They could still hear the faint growl of its engine. Then she picked up a stick and swung it hard to make a swishing noise.

"He came riding from that way," she said, pointing with the stick. "He rode widdershins, probably around the whole thing. Checking for breaks. Patching them up. Maintaining one big, banishing circle around the town." She rolled her wrist as though the stick were a sword. Then she tossed it aside.

"How is he still alive?" Jasper asked. "I know that mustache. It's everywhere. In portraits. Up on the wall of the post office, and in the bank, and in the library. But Barron would have to be a hundred and fifty years old by now."

"Let's go ask him," Rosa said. She marched down the trail.

Jasper hoisted his quarterstaff and scrambled to keep up. "You know where he's going?"

"Home, probably."

"The library was a manor house, before it was a library," Jasper said. "His house. Which I know, because I am very well versed in matters of local history." He took on a tone of exaggerated self-importance, one that Sir Dad often used.

"And the tree said she had come home to claim him when she went rampaging at the library," Rosa said.

"So the tree was Isabelle Barron."

"Seems likely," said Rosa.

The two hurried down the mountainside, farther away from the circle's edge. Seething anger seeped out of them.

Jasper felt better.

Rosa didn't. She would rather have stayed angry. Mom's voice was still stuck on the other side, held close by a ghost in a gown of ashes. Rosa didn't want to leave it there. But she also knew what always happened to banishment circles—and to everything inside them.

17

BEHIND THE LIBRARY THEY FOUND A RICKETY gardening shed. It was locked, but it had a small window. Through the window they saw the old motorcycle.

"Have you poked around the rest of the library much?" Jasper whispered. "How many apartments are there in the basement?"

"Just ours," Rosa whispered back. "But I don't think we should look down." She watched the upper windows for light and movement. Tower rooms jutted above the rooftop as though the library were a small castle of red brick. "I think we should look up."

They paused in the front lobby to admire the

mustache in Barron's ornate portrait. Then they walked casually inside.

"We're just here to borrow some books," Jasper said. He felt a little bit conspicuous to be armed with a quarterstaff. "That's all we're doing here. I'm going to look at the pitiful shelf of graphic novels, even though I've read them all and only two of them are any good. La la la."

Rosa hitched up her tool belt. "I live here," she said. "I don't need an excuse. So I'm just coming home. Yep. That's all I'm doing."

The front desk was empty. The whole place seemed to be empty—which was strange for the middle of the day, in the middle of the summer. No one else was there to notice the innocent and nonchalant performance.

Rosa led the way into Special Collections, which was also empty. But then they heard someone descend the forbidden staircase, so they ducked underneath a table.

Mrs. Jillynip came down the spiral stairs. She held a tray covered with a cloth. The tray made small, sharp noises like empty dishes clinking together as she carried it, with utmost care and deliberate, frustrating slowness, through Special Collections and away.

Rosa and Jasper peeked out from underneath the table.

"I'm amazed she carried food and drink in here," Rosa whispered. "Not supposed to do that."

They scrambled for the stairs. Jasper tried to hold the quarterstaff with care, but it still knocked against the steps a couple of times.

"Shhhhh!"

"Sorry!"

At the top they found a fancy, filthy set of rooms. The air smelled thick, like mildew or the pages of unloved books. Dusty sunlight broke through leaded windows and then got lost in the piles of odd instruments, stacks of paper scribbled over with mathematical calculations and Greek incantations, and furniture that used to be luxurious before it got forgotten, left to rot beneath the stacks and piles of other things.

Rosa spotted several trophies with little brass swordsmen at the top. *A fencing master*, she thought. *No wonder he's good with boundaries and circles.*

A tall and slender man stood hunched over a table, examining a map. His mustache trailed down below his face and rustled against the paper. He did not notice that he had visitors. And Rosa was not sure how to address the ancient founder of Ingot Town.

"Mr. Barron?" she finally said.

The old man stood up straight, peered through the dusty light, and noticed them.

"Miss Díaz." His voice felt like genteel sandpaper in her ears. "Welcome. I would offer you refreshment, but I have supped just now and the dear Widow Jillynip already cleared it all away. But do please join me for conversation. Will you sit?" He looked around. "I did have chairs here once. They may have broken. Or else I might have removed all the copper fittings and put them to new purposes. That seems likely. My apologies. I hope that you do not mind standing." He moved aside to make room at the table. "Is your mother with you? No? Still convalescing? No matter. I'll speak to her later. And we have so very much work to do that this cannot wait."

Rosa and Jasper both felt like they had skipped a few pages. Neither one of them knew how to catch up. They stood close, side by side, and approached together.

The map on the table displayed the whole valley of Ingot—including an X marked "Barron Copper Mine" at the southernmost end of Isabelle Road. A circle drawn in bright green ink cut off that road near the X. The circle surrounded the whole town and valley. A thick green dot marked the library in the very center.

"We have so very much to do," Barron said again, and tapped at the map with the tip of a ruler. "This is why I brought you here, Miss Díaz. This is why I sent for you."

18

ROSA CROSSED HER ARMS. "YOU BROUGHT US HERE."

"I did." Barron bent down to peer at the details of his map. He looked like a stork hunting for frogs. "I did. I am still on the board of this library. I'm on the board of *most* institutions hereabouts, of course, though I have so little time for the meetings. And now I find myself in dire need of assistance, so I made certain that the library hired the best specialist they could find. And by bringing your mother here we also got *you* thrown into the bargain—a smaller specialist of no small accomplishment. That was a fine piece of luck. I congratulate you on your fairground efforts. They did ultimately fail, but you had very little warning or opportunity to prepare. I am still impressed." He cracked long knuckles on his long fingers. His voice seemed to stretch and elongate the time it took for him to speak. "I am likewise impressed that the two of you were able to approach my barrier this morning. That showed extraordinary strength of will."

Oops. "You saw us," Jasper said.

Barron hesitated, just a little, and when he spoke he addressed Rosa. "I did see you. And I am sorry that I did not offer you a ride back into town, but my sidecar was too cluttered for passengers. Besides, you were hiding. I did not want to make you feel foolish by pointing out your inadequate stealth. Dear Isabelle and myself never had children, but while on holiday I played hide-and-seek with my sister's sons. I never found them as quickly as I could have. I let them think themselves more clever than they were in fact. That gave them confidence. Very important. I hope you are feeling confident as well. Now to business."

Jasper and Rosa looked at each other sideways. They both wanted to laugh, or yell, or turn right around and leave. But they forced themselves to play along.

"What business did you have in mind, sir?" Rosa's words were respectful thorns on the stem of her voice.

"Our business, of course," Barron said with a sandpapery chuckle. "The business of dealing with ghosts.

I keep the town safe from hauntings. But now my boundary is wearing down. They have begun to break through. Your cute little tricks of chalk and salt might help slow down intrusions, however, and that would give me time to repair every breach as it occurs. Most of them occur right here." He tapped one thick finger at the bottom of Isabelle Road. "Right where you hid yourselves earlier."

"Right where we saw Isabelle herself," Rosa said.

"Did you?" Barron asked, but it was the opposite of a question. His tone chased away answers rather than asking for them. "Did you? Well. Yes. Well. Anything you can do at that spot would be very much appreciated. Meanwhile, I will continue to patch and patrol along the entire border. I have enlisted others to help me do this, and given them the means to approach that boundary. A first, for me. This has always been my undertaking, and mine alone. But no longer."

Rosa felt her patience slip away. "Why did you make the border in the first place?" Barron dug at his inner ear with a long pinky finger and pretended not to hear the question, so Rosa asked again. "Sir? Why did you build that circle?"

"I am protecting Ingot." Barron's slow voice hardened, but he tried to slap a shiny gilt of kindness on it.

"Yes," Rosa agreed. "You're protecting Ingot from

dangers you created, and ghosts that you banished. But why did you banish them? How did this whole doomed project get started?"

"Oh, no, no, no," Barron said. "These efforts are not doomed, my dear child. I have maintained a functioning border between the living and the dead for ten times the span of your life thus far. I can maintain it for longer yet."

"Not very much longer," Rosa insisted. "Banishment leads to backlash. And the longer you keep it going, the worse the lashing out will be. You've kept your circle closed for a pretty long time—"

"Yes," he said, proud and smug. "I have."

He wasn't listening. Rosa tried harder.

"—so, when it finally collapses, it will kill every single living thing in this valley. Then the old ghosts and the new ones will circle each other, howling, for the next thousand years at least. Ingot will be home to nothing and no one but bare rock and screams."

"Really?" Jasper whispered.

"Yeah," Rosa said. "Really."

Jasper tried to digest this. His bracelet felt uncomfortably warm.

Barron just blinked at Rosa, stunned. Then he chuckled. "Aren't we the little pessimist? I am gratified, however, that you understand the importance of our work."

"This isn't *our* work!" Rosa shouted, louder than she meant to be. She tried to hold her temper close and not let it fly around the room. "This isn't *my* work. This is banishment, and banishment *doesn't* work. You can't keep that circle whole. It isn't possible."

"Ah," Barron said. "But all technical feats and accomplishments are considered impossible, at least until someone like me finally achieves them. And I confess that I have never understood the difference between banishment and appeasement, apart from the weakness of the word 'appease.' It smacks of cautious timidity and surrender, don't you think?"

Rosa didn't, and tried to say so, but Barron's voice rolled right over her.

"Surely our work is the same," he said. "You deal with ghosts. I deal with ghosts. The only fundamental difference, as far as I can see, is that my methods are much more effective, and they last. Will you assist me, and save Ingot, or will you waste more time quibbling?"

He took a small glass from the table and sipped. He didn't seem to notice that the glass was empty, and also broken. Neither did he notice when he cut one finger on the jagged edge.

Barron's blood dripped green from his hand to the map below.

19

ROSA BACKED AWAY SLOWLY.

Jasper lifted his quarterstaff.

Barron sipped a drink that was not there.

"Well?" he asked. "Please don't disappoint me, child."

"I'll check in with Mom," she said, pleased at how steady her own voice sounded. "I'll see what we have handy for those cute little appeasement tricks."

"I am very much obliged," Barron said, and turned back to his map.

Rosa and Jasper bolted down the stairs. This time they didn't care how much clattering noise they made.

"He's dead!" Rosa whisper-shouted as soon as they

reached the bottom. "He's already dead! Going through all his old motions. And talking a lot. I've never heard a ghost talk so much. The voices usually fade. Plus they're stuck with whatever words they said out loud while they were living. Sometimes I say random words, a whole bunch of them, just to make sure I'll have them later. He must have really loved the sound of his own voice when he was still alive. I wonder when he died. I wonder if he even *noticed* when it happened. And why is he bleeding green? Never seen anything bleed green before. Mom probably has. But I can't ask her about it. I mean, I can *ask*, but she can't give me any answers."

"Shhhh," Jasper shushed.

"Don't shush me, knight."

"Copper," he said.

"What about copper?" she demanded. "Barron had a copper mine down at the end of Isabelle Road. Said so on his map. Plus the name of this stupid town is a pretty sizable hint. Local ghosts are practically allergic to copper. But he isn't. He's okay with stealing pipe fixtures from the bathrooms here and patching up his huge circle. He doesn't mind copper. But why is his blood green?"

"I think he's *made out of copper*." Jasper turned to face the staircase behind them, just in case Barron followed them down. "He's bleeding copper. Using it instead of iron. We bleed red. The iron in our blood gets rusty when it hits the air. But copper rusts green."

"Oh," Rosa said. "Okay."

"That's why Mars is red," he went on. "Lots of iron."

"Got it," she said.

"Did you hear about the ghost rivers that Curiosity found on Mars?" he asked.

"Stop talking about Mars!"

"Shhhhh," said Mrs. Jillynip behind them. "This is a library, children."

Rosa spun around and very nearly knocked over a stack of rolled-up maps. "You knew," she said. "You knew about Barron."

Mrs. Jillynip sniffed. "It is my job to know about him, and to offer him refreshment. Or appeasement, if you like. A little offering of milk and honey. And I would have thought that a city librarian with your vast experience of hauntings wouldn't be so troubled by one well-respected ghost in our attic. I do hope you haven't upset him. I asked you not to go upstairs."

"He's banished all of the others," Rosa tried to explain, but Mrs. Jillynip wasn't having it.

"Go and play somewhere else, the both of you. Children are not permitted in Special Collections. You didn't sign the clipboard. You are not wearing gloves.

And try not to bump any shelves with that stick. Go on."

She shooed them out and shut the door in their faces.

Rosa didn't move. She just stood and stared at the door.

"What now?" Jasper asked.

"I didn't get groceries," she said softly. "I was supposed to get groceries. We don't have much in the kitchen. And we skipped lunch. I forgot all about the existence of lunch. Mom is probably hungry. She couldn't get groceries. She can't read labels anymore. She doesn't have a voice, not even inside her own head. We should go get her. And get some food. Plus this building is the precise center of one great big bubble of banishment, and that bubble is going to pop. Soon. So we should probably leave."

"Probably," Jasper agreed.

Rosa didn't move.

"Is your Mom downstairs?" he prompted.

"Yeah," Rosa said.

"Show me. I didn't know this place had a basement."

Rosa made herself move. She led the way to the door and the stairs in the back, and down they went.

20

JASPER THOUGHT THE DOWNSTAIRS APARTMENT was kind of fantastic.

"It's a whole set of secret rooms!"

"It's a cave," said Rosa. She did not think that this was a good thing, but Jasper did.

"Exactly. A secret cave. It's so quiet down here."

"Of course it's quiet," she said. "We're underground, beneath a library, in isolated little Ingot. I miss noise. I miss traffic and people outside."

"We should switch places," Jasper suggested. "Dad's rumbling voice sounds like traffic, and it fills up the whole house. So does his snoring." They peered around piles of boxes. "Where's your mom?"

"Mom!" Rosa called, even though she already knew that her mother couldn't answer.

They climbed over the couch on their way to the kitchen, where they found her. She was slowly unpacking her tool belt and spreading the contents across the kitchen table.

"Hi Mom," Rosa said. "Why are you . . . never mind. We need to go. We need to find some food. And we need to figure out what to do before the wall between the living and the dead collapses."

Athena Díaz the appeasement specialist did not respond. Instead she set a candle stub at one end of the round table, and another stub at the opposite end. It looked like she was playing chess against herself on a chessboard that made no sense.

"Mom?" Rosa asked quietly. "Come on. We need to leave. We need to be away from this library before a host of vengeful dead come howling down the mountainside. We need to undo a hundred years of banishment without killing the whole town. I don't know how to do that. I don't think *anyone* knows how to do that. Except you. Maybe. But you can't tell me. And I'm hungry. We should go. Right this very now."

Mom moved more of the tabletop mess around.

"Look at me," Rosa pleaded.

Her mother looked up at her, but Rosa couldn't read

that look. Then Mom took the two candle stubs and set each one on the rim of a coffee mug. Rosa bit the inside of her cheek, hard.

Jasper picked up a folded photograph from the mess. "Who's this?"

She glanced at the picture. "That was my dad." It wasn't the best picture of him, though. He looked all serious. Whenever Rosa imagined her father he wore his "oops" sort of smile.

"He's dead?" Jasper asked carefully.

"He's dead," Rosa told him, her voice as flat as she could make it. "He wasn't . . . very good at the family business. I covered for him when he messed up. Which was a lot. Then he transferred to a tiny little library across town. Barely haunted, as libraries go, so he really should have been able to handle the place. He should have known better."

"Better than what?" Jasper asked. "What did he do?"

"He banished a poltergeist that he couldn't appease. It flattened that whole building trying to come home. And Dad was in the building. Now it's just a gravel pit. The poltergeist is still there. It tosses the gravel around. Banishment doesn't work. It doesn't ever work."

Jasper had a thought that Rosa probably wouldn't like. "People who move to Ingot usually have a reason."

Rosa understood, and didn't like it. "You mean they're haunted by something they can't appease? So they come to get unhaunted. Disinfected. Like a stack of old library books here on loan." She folded the picture of her father back up. "Mom hasn't been herself. Not since he died. But he wouldn't haunt us. He wouldn't do that to us. And Mom would know how to handle it, even if he did. Plus I haven't seen him. I would have seen him, right? In the mirror, at least. I would have seen him when I put pebbles on the mirror shelves, if he was there. If he was haunting us. Right? Wouldn't I?"

Rosa wasn't sure which one of them she was trying convince.

Mom didn't respond to the conversation. She kept her head down and continued to move things around the table. She set a candle stub on the edge of a plate. Then she set another candle on the opposite edge.

Jasper started to speak, but Rosa waved a hand at him. "Shut up."

"I'm only . . ."

"Shush! Shush, shush, shush. Just watch."

Mom reached into an open cardboard box and pulled out the lid to their pressure cooker. She did not look up. She did not do anything communicative in Rosa's direction. She just set the lid on the table and put two candles on the rim.

Jasper caught on. "Circles."

"Circles," Rosa agreed. "She's putting candles on the edges of a bunch of round things."

Mom stopped fiddling with stuff on the table. She still didn't look up, but she did look satisfied.

"Okay," Jasper said. "Meaning what?"

Rosa clapped her hands and rubbed them together. "There's a whole lot of pressure bearing down on Barron's copper circle. It gets worse whenever someone here dies. Or looks in a mirror. Or goes through a doorway. Or does anything else that would brush up against ghosts in a properly haunted place. And that pressure will just keep building up until—boom. Collapse. Backlash and awfulness. But maybe we can ease the pressure if we invite them back in. Slooooooowly. With candles. Big ones." She looked up with hope and mischief. "Know where we can find a couple of really big candles?"

21

ROSA RUSHED THEM OUT THE DOOR, DOWN THE front steps, and onto the sidewalk. The cement was still charred where the tree had collapsed.

"Mom, do you think you can drive? It isn't very far. You wouldn't have to read street signs. And you can't yell at everyone else on the road the way you usually do, but do you think maybe you can still drive a little ways?"

Her mother did not respond, and probably would not have responded even if she had a voice. Instead she led the way to their rusty little car in the back of the library parking lot. They all climbed in.

A medallion of Patron Francesca Romana dangled from their review mirror. This was a sign of respect for highway spirits, and for the ghosts that lurk inside used car parts.

Rosa thought about the ghosts that used to lurk inside this one. They would have been ripped away as soon as the car reached Ingot, through the highway tunnel and underneath the copper circle on the mountainside. Now all of those little ghosts were stuck on the far side of that barrier, along with the spirit of each haunted thing that Rosa had brought here—every book, every relic, every used piece of clothing. All of her familiar haints were there on the mountain, displaced and disoriented.

Along with her father. Maybe. Even though they had already settled what was left of him into a memorial lantern behind their old library, so he really shouldn't have followed them here.

They reached the fairgrounds. Tree-smashed cars still littered the parking lot, which was mostly empty otherwise. Ms. Díaz drove carefully across the mud, flattened grass, and fragments of windshield to park near the front gate.

The gate was shut. The festival was officially closed, although a sign in hastily painted calligraphy promised A GRANDE REOPENING ON THE MORROW!!!

Rosa hoped that Ingot would last until tomorrow.

Her stomach growled, long and low.

"Let's head for the tavern first," Jasper suggested. "Mr. Rathaus is probably 'helping' the repair work by staying open and selling us the same overpriced, over-cooked food he sells to tourists."

They picked their way through the wall wreckage where the stampeding tree had passed yesterday, then found the Tacky Tavern. Ms. Díaz bought turkey legs. Rosa helped her count out the bills, since Mom couldn't currently read the numbers. Then they all gnawed on the leg bones of turkeys. This was satisfying, even though the meat didn't taste like much.

Rosa watched festival folk while she chewed. They wore half-costumes and carried power tools. Buzz saws buzzed and drill bits whined. Smashed stalls got sorted into piles of salvageable and unsalvageable things. A girl repainted the carved wooden sign for YE OLDE CAP-PUCCINOS with slow and deliberate care. A man sat under a tree and plucked out a skipping sort of tune on a battered lute. He wore denim and only denim, the blue jeans and button-up shirt both faded to the same gray-ish color as his beard. It made him look like an old gray fox, temporarily human-shaped so he could use fingers. The musician didn't seem to mind that the power tools were louder than his song.

Rosa listened. In that moment she understood why Ingot had the biggest and best Renaissance Festival to be found anywhere. That understanding hurt.

Oh, she thought. *This is what happens to an unhaunted place.*

The town might not know what it had lost, or why it was gone, but Ingot pressed against that absence like a tongue where a lost tooth used to be. Starved of history, they patched together new echoes from mismatched fragments. Unhaunted, they learned how to haunt themselves.

This is a funeral, she realized. *This is a wake. They hold it every summer, all summer long, to mourn a history they don't have and don't even remember losing.* It was futile, and flailing, and goofy, and hopeless, and beautiful.

The musician played on. He would probably keep playing when Barron's circle broke and all the ghosts came howling home.

22

SIR MORIEN STRODE INTO THE TAVERN. HE WORE full armor, of course, even though this was an informal day of rehearsals and repairs. All eyes turned to him, just like they always did. He prepared to spin gold from their attention.

Jasper winced, hunched his shoulders, and wished he could crawl under the table without anyone noticing.

"What's going on?" Rosa asked around a mouthful of tasteless turkey.

"A morale-boosting speech," he told her.

"But it probably won't boost *your* morale," she said.

"Probably not."

Sir Dad climbed onto the bar, cleared his throat, and stomped one foot.

Uncle Fox stopped playing his tune. Nearby power tools all hushed.

"Our revels have not ended!" Sir Dad roared. "The spirits that disturbed this festive ground have burned away and melted into air. Such denizens may still return, and yet upstage this humble festival—"

Jasper snorted. He couldn't take this speechifying seriously. None of Dad's endeavors were ever humble. But no one else took it seriously, either—and neither did Dad. He pushed his goofball approximation of old chivalry right through silliness and out the other side, to a place that wasn't serious but carried the same weight.

"We will not lock our gates, or flee the field like horses driven wild. Sing while you toil. Strike up a tune. Strike nails with hammers to keep proper time. Today we must restore our pageantry!"

The crowd cheered, and started singing. Of course they did.

Sir Dad climbed down from the bar and set out to boost morale elsewhere.

Jasper sat up a little straighter.

"That was fun," Rosa said.

"Yeah," said Jasper. "Fun."

"He was the one in the spotlight," Rosa pointed out. "Not you."

"Always feels like it's me." He tossed his turkey bone into a barrel. "Come on. We should hurry before someone tries to put us to work."

Rosa took one last bite and ditched the rest. "Mom, are you comfortable enough right here? We'll be back soon. Hopefully."

Mom did not answer, unless putting her feet up on the neighboring bench was a kind of answer.

Rosa and Jasper left the tavern.

"We should find more copper," she said. "If there is any of the stuff left."

"Try Nell's smithy," he said, pointing. "Tell her I sent you. I'll go talk to Duncan at the Waxworks. He can be a little persnickety."

The two split up on their separate errands.

Duncan Barnstaple, master candlemaker, labored in a haze of wood smoke and beeswax. He seemed to be melting down broken candles and returning them to the bubbling, primordial ooze from whence they came.

He did not wear contemporary clothing, even on an informal day of repairs and rehearsals. He wore period clothes beneath a leather apron, and braided his long, blond beard to keep strands from dropping into the wax. Duncan the candlemaker believed in *authenticity*. He refused to see or acknowledge anachronisms, and would ignore anything spoken out of character.

Jasper took a moment to find his accent. "Good morrow to you, master craftsman."

The candlemaker looked up from his cauldron. "And to you, noble squire. What business brings you here with such clear urgency?"

"A knightly business," Jasper said. "To defend the good people of Ingot from harm."

Duncan nodded, approving. "Such is your profession."

"And to accomplish this, we find ourselves in dire need of *your* profession."

"Strange." The candlemaker stirred his molten wax. "How may I serve this knightly business?"

"We require candles. Two of them, and both of a prodigious size. At least an ell in height."

Duncan pulled at his braided beard. "I have such candles here. They once burned within the sanctuary of libraries, to assist the twilit studies of the patrons there. They are impressive. And most expensive. Note that I have carved the hours, and verses of old poems, into the sides of each."

"This is fine work," Jasper agreed. "But do you have plain, unfinished candles that you might willingly part with? Misshapen, even?"

Duncan made a face as though Jasper had sneezed on his dinner and refused to apologize. "Misshapen? I would be loath to allow apprentice-level work to leave my shop."

Jasper tried not to let his impatience come blazing out of his face. *I wish the Fantastical Candle stall was still here,* he thought. *I could have just said, "Hey, do you have anything really, really tall? It doesn't need to look fancy."* He swallowed bile and tried to be convincing.

"I swear by your beard, master of the waxworks, that this is urgent and no slight to your craft."

Duncan considered his beard a very potent thing to swear by. "I had intended to melt down a pair of cracked sanctuary candles," he said. "I may be willing to give them to you instead. But first explain your urgency."

Jasper hesitated, and then dove right in. "My friend and I intend to breach a misguided and unnatural barrier that stands between the living and the dead."

"Ah." Duncan considered this. He decided that he would rather not know any more about it. "Very well."

23

ROSA FOUND NELL MACMINNIGAN LABORING OVER
the forge. A rope fence kept everyone else away from
this dangerous, clanging activity. Rosa ducked right
under the rope.

Nell stopped hitting metal things together. "I
thought people in your line of work respected boundaries," she said.

"Usually," said Rosa, pleased to be recognized.
"We're also pretty good at breaking them."

"So I see." Nell wiped her brow with a sooty fore-
arm. "What can I do for you, specialist?"

"I need a little copper," Rosa said. "Ideally something
wearable. Jasper said the two of you talked about the stuff."

"We did. Here, follow me." The smith took off her heavy gloves and went to the very back of the smithy. Rosa followed. "I don't have much. And you're not the first to ask. Englebert and his ghost-hunting militia came by earlier with lumps of raw copper around their necks, and they wanted more."

"There's a ghost-hunting militia?" Rosa asked. "That's a terrible idea."

"I know it," said Nell. "Idiots of Ingot are wearing ingots as jewelry and wielding arcane weaponry. Last night they kept close to the festival, marching around and trying to intimidate trees into holding still. But now they're gone. Not sure where they went. That makes me nervous. And here you come, making similar requests for wearable metal. Makes me even more nervous. Local ghosts are not fond of copper, correct?"

"Not at all," Rosa said. "Practically allergic to it."

"Why is that, do you think?"

Rosa hesitated. "The town doesn't really want to remember where it came from."

Nell made a thoughtful noise. "Think you can help? You and your mother?"

Yes, Rosa thought. *Maybe. Hopefully. If Mom's idea works. And I really don't know if it's going to work. I've used candles to give ghosts a place to keep warm and be remembered. I've coaxed little bathroom spirits across mirrors with candles. But I've never done anything like this.*

She wanted to trust her mother. She wanted unshaken and unshakable faith in Athena Díaz and her legendary appeasement skills. But Rosa didn't have that faith anymore. She needed to learn how to keep moving without it.

"Yes," she said. "I think so."

"Right then." Nell pulled a blanket covering away from a low table.

A sword lay across that table. It was short, only about two feet long, but with a wide blade. The burnished metal glowed richly orange and brown.

"Wow," Rosa said.

She picked it up. Nell didn't stop her, though she did watch her very carefully.

"This right here is the best Bronze Age work I've ever done," she said. "I'd finished the recasso blade already, and then set it aside. Most sword collectors are looking for something more recent and renaissancy. But then young Jasper clued me in to the whole copper thing. Bronze is *mostly* copper. Almost entirely. So I came back to this blade, and finished the hilt. What do you think?"

"It's so light." Rosa rolled her wrist in a slow moùliné, testing the weight of it.

"Very," Nell said. "Heavy blades are overrated. Good for chopping wood and little else. Hard to recover after a swing."

Rosa examined the blade. "Is it Llyn Fawr style?"

Nell grinned. "No, but close. This one is more Ewart Park-ish. You know your swords."

Rosa nodded. "I've always lived in libraries." She set the weapon back on the table. "But I didn't come to you for this sort of thing. We're not going to pick a fight."

Nell's grin got wider. "I like that. Very much. Because I'm not interested in helping *anyone* pick a fight. Certainly not the ghost-hunting boys who've taken up arms. But you . . . I watched you bring a stampeding tree to a standstill yesterday by drawing shapes in the dirt with a pocketknife. You've got skills —the sorts of skills that the rest of us here in Ingot just don't have. So take the sword. *Not* to pick a fight. Just to set boundaries around you. If you need it."

Rosa paused. She waited for Nell to change her mind, or say *Just kidding*.

"Take it," Nell said instead. "As a saleswoman, it pains me when somebody buys the wrong thing. I'll sell it to them anyway, because I need groceries. But it physically hurts to see somebody hold a blade that is very obviously wrong for them. This one is obviously yours. Take it."

Rosa took it. She buckled the leather sheath to her tool belt between the matches and the pouch of salt. The weight of it felt new and strange, but it also felt like it belonged there.

Nell rubbed calloused hands together. "Excellent. As for wearable stuff, I have a few bracelets and armlets like mine. Take them. But I would like you to bring them back again."

"I will," Rosa promised. "But don't you want to know what we're up to, before you let me walk away with your merchandise?"

"Not really," Nell said. "I'd rather keep clear of ghostly things and let you handle knowing about them. Need anything else?"

Rosa suddenly felt like she had swallowed an extra dose of awkward. "There is one more thing. I hate to ask, but could you maybe help babysit my mom?"

24

THE SUN WAS SETTING ALREADY. HIGH MOUNTAINS
raised up the horizon and brought early sunsets down.

Rosa and Jasper left the Renaissance Festival, each
with a huge candle under one arm. Rosa had gouged the
word Αλήθεια, over and over again, into both pillars of
wax.

"Aletheia" meant truth, revealed and remembered.
It was a word that washed "lethe" away.

"People are going to be mad about this," Jasper
mused.

"Probably," Rosa agreed.

"Really mad. Panicked mad. We've never had to
deal with ghosts before."

"Nope," said Rosa.

"Plus a bunch of them came here to get away from hauntings. What if their old ghosts find them again? What if—"

He stopped, suddenly, and swallowed the rest.

What if Mom was haunted? Rosa thought. *Maybe she couldn't handle it at the time. Maybe that's why we moved here. And maybe she'll be haunted again if we do this.*

"The ghosts are all coming back anyway," she said aloud. "They'll break through. Soon. But if this works then they won't flatten everyone and everything else when they come."

"Think it'll work?" Jasper asked.

"Yes," Rosa said. "Kinda. Maybe. Hopefully."

"Good enough." He hoisted up the candle. It was already getting heavy.

"You remember what to do?" Rosa asked. "Run through it one more time."

"Go north," Jasper said. "Get to the big copper circle. Put the candle on it. Light the candle. Invite the ghosts to come home. Stand out of their way when they do."

"That last part is *really* important," Rosa said. "They've been stuck for a long time. They might lash out, even if invited. Make yourself a circle. Use salt. Do you have enough salt?"

Jasper produced a handful of paper salt packets, newly swiped from the Tacky Tavern.

"And those new bracelets fit?"

"They seem to." He fiddled with the studded leather things around his wrists. "They look silly, though. Makes me feel like I should be wearing a leather jacket and riding a Harley."

"Yeah," Rosa agreed. "They kinda do. But the extra copper should make it easier for you to climb the hill and get close to the wall. Don't forget to breathe when you start to get angry."

"I won't."

They reached the road. Jasper looked north. Rosa looked south. She switched her candle from her right arm to her left. "I wish we could do this together. But we need to light these at pretty much the same time. And they need to be at opposite ends. Otherwise we'll collapse the circle too quickly. That would be bad. Do you have enough salt?"

He didn't bother answering. "Thanks for doing all this," he said. "Thanks for defending a place you hate."

"I don't hate it," Rosa said, and surprised herself by saying so. "I don't like it much," she admitted, "but I think I understand it better. And it's about to change."

"Do you know *how* it'll change?" he asked. "If this works? Do you know what Ingot will be like?"

"No," Rosa said. "But it will be haunted. Just like everywhere else."

Jasper tried to picture his hometown as a haunted place.

"Probably more so than everywhere else," she added.

He gave up even trying to picture it. Jasper had never lived anywhere else.

"Good luck," he said, and set out northward.

Rosa waved. Then she hiked south along Isabelle Road.

She passed the point where the road ended, and all of the signs warning swimmers away from the poisoned pond. DO NOT SWIM. DO NOT DRINK. WATER UNSAFE. NO FISHING. NO HUNTING. NO TRESPASSING.

Rosa picked up a rock and threw it into the sickly looking water. She tried to throw all of her doubts along with it.

"Hi Dad," she said.

The stone made an oozing sort of splash.

Her medallion and armlet began to feel cold.

25

JASPER WALKED ALL THE WAY THROUGH TOWN,
just as he had yesterday. But this time he walked alone,
without Sir Dad in the lead. He hoped no neighbors
would notice him, try to strike up a conversation, or ask
why he lugged a large candle around.

Most would probably take issue with what Jasper
meant to accomplish with that candle.

He left the sidewalks and struck out through the
northern foothills. No one ever came this way. Jasper
hiked without a clear path or trail. He pushed through
brush and scratching branches.

The bracelets grew cold against his wrists. He tried
singing *"The Ballad of the Hapless Highwayman"* just

to distract himself. It was one of Sir Dad's favorites, and Dad's voice made panic impossible. Jasper's voice cracked a little. Dad would have relished the chance to ride off on a knightly errand. Jasper felt more and more foolish the farther he climbed. He tried to embrace that foolish feeling. He sang louder about the misadventures of the very worst robber to ever rob highways. But the song dwindled and fizzled by the time he reached Barron's circle and the roiling wall of fog.

A motor rumbled close by. Jasper heard wheels on Barron's track, and froze. *It's him*, he thought. *Crap, crap, crap. Dead man Barron is riding this way on his motorcycle.* But it wasn't Barron. Four mopeds came racing around the bend instead, all four ridden by festival folk.

Englebert the stable boy rode in the lead. He held a guisarme—a big spear with extra hooks and spikes all over it, clearly forged by Mr. Smoot. The guisarme balanced awkwardly against the handlebars.

Humphrey the Victorian rode with his ornate flame-thrower strapped to his back.

Two spear-carrying members of the royal guard brought up the rear.

The ghost-hunting militia braked their mopeds and dismounted. All of them wore lumps of copper on necklace chains. All of them looked twitchy with rage that they didn't understand.

"We know what you're doing," Englebert said. He practically shouted the words. "We can't let you do it. We have to defend Ingot from the dead."

Rosa stood beside the copper barrier, her toes almost touching it. "Lethe," it said, over and over again, etched into metal.

She scratched Ἀλήθεια into the side of a wooden match with the point of a needle. Probably unnecessary. The word was already all over the candle itself. But she wanted to be sure. This was the place closest to the copper mine, the part of the circle that had broken yesterday. This would take extra care.

Rosa took the travel mug and used her salty compass to pick the precise spot. She lit the memorial candle, held it sideways, and dripped hot wax over fused copper bathroom fixtures. Then she stuck the base of the candle to the dribbled pool of molten wax.

Mist swirled in darker colors behind it.

"Come in," Rosa said. "We're inviting you in. We're inviting you home."

The wick burned orange, and then it burned green.

Rosa let herself believe that this might work.

A wind rose up around her. The temperature dropped.

Bartholomew Theosophras Barron came riding up

the path. He dismounted from his motorcycle. Green candlelight reflected in his eyes.

"You will not do this, child," said Barron's ghost.

Rosa drew her sword.

Jasper set the candle on the ground and stood beside it.

The militia fanned out around him. He was the center of their vengeful attention.

He hated being the center of attention.

I don't know how to handle this, he admitted to himself. *Dad would know, but I don't.* He felt a brief, bright flash of resentment for his father and the easy way he seemed to handle every kind of scrutiny. Jasper wasn't sure how much of that resentment was his own, and how much he borrowed from behind the wall.

I'm not my dad, he thought. *But I can play him. I can borrow some confidence that isn't really mine.*

Jasper shifted his posture to stand like Sir Dad.

Look at me. Listen to me. It is right and fitting that I should have your attention.

"You're trying to defend our town," he said to the other boys. "Good. Thank you. But you have this whole entire situation backwards."

"We stood safe for a hundred years inside this circle," Englebert said. He clearly meant to sound brave, but his voice whined and undermined him. "The town founder told us so. Now some girl swoops in from the city to say we've been doing it all wrong?"

"She knows her business," Jasper said simply.

"But she doesn't know ours," Englebert insisted. "A haunted Ingot won't be Ingot anymore."

"Then we will mourn what it used to be," Jasper said, his father's cadence in his own voice. His imaginary confidence started to feel solid and real. "We will also live to recognize what else it might become."

"Stop that!" Englebert shouted, spit flying. Jasper heard something else riding alongside that rage. "Stop pretending! You're not a knight. You aren't doing anything noble. We are. We're noble. And we're not going to let you do this."

Jasper watched the others who stood behind the stable boy. They looked both determined and uncomfortable.

He glanced at the wall, where fog rolled, roiled, and pushed against the line it could not cross. Dried leaves crackled near the copper barrier as frost covered them.

Maybe I can reach it, he thought. *If I run. Maybe I can dodge between them, get this massive, awkward candle where it needs to go, and then light the Zippo. Sure.*

He knew that he couldn't, but he gathered himself up to try it. Then his sense of time shifted.

Everything happened slowly, each action distinct and separate from every other action.

Humphrey pointed a gear-encrusted hose at the sky and let loose a warning burst of flame.

Englebert held up his weapon in a menacing way. He held it *entirely* wrong.

Behind their posturing the copper barrier cracked. Mist leaked though the breach. Cold air tickled at the back of Jasper's teeth and made his breath catch.

Too late, he thought.

He whacked the ground hard with the tip of his staff, drew a wide circle around himself, and threw down salt.

Then the dead broke through.

Rosa stood with her back to the wall. She used her sword to draw a hasty half-circle around the candle and herself.

She had only enough room for a half-circle.

"An incomplete shape will not hold, child," Barron said. He said it kindly, as though offering her helpful advice. Then he blew the candle out from several feet away.

Her left hand fumbled at her belt pouch for a handful of salt. She got the clasp open and scattered the stuff in front of her. "You still can't step over this."

Barron drew a rusty fencing foil from the mess of

scrap metal in his sidecar. "I have no need to step across your awkward line in the dirt. I only need to reach over it to dismember that ungainly memorial candle. Please stand aside."

Rosa took up a fighting stance instead.

"Ah." Barron smiled. His smile looked grotesque. "To the death? No. Redundant. To your honor, then, and my own." He offered a formal salute with his rusting sword.

Rosa returned the salute. She wanted to say something brave and clever, but she didn't have time. He attacked. She parried in a quick, panicked reflex.

You know how to do this, she insisted to herself. *Remember how to do this. You used to duel with Mom all the time.* But she had never crossed swords with a dead banishment specialist before.

Barron attacked again. She parried again, moving hastily as though trying to swat a zigzagging fly.

"Surrender," he said. "Your art is made of compromise and embarrassment. Mine reshapes the world and its possibilities according to my stronger will. And I will not yield. I will not be appeased. I will maintain the wall around Ingot Town."

He struck high, low, and to the center. He moved in straight lines. Ghosts often do.

Rosa offered parry, remedy, and counter. She moved

in arcs. The tip of her bronze blade marked the outer circle of her farthest reach, and she shifted her stance to expand that reach.

Barron struck as though chopping wood. Whackity, whackity, hack. High, low, and to the center. Again. Always. He fought in echoes, stuck in the endless loop of a compulsive haunting. He moved in patterns doomed to repeat.

Breathe, Rosa thought. *Don't forget to breathe.*

Barron attacked. She didn't bother to parry the rusty foil this time. Instead she just stepped aside, and cut off Barron's hand at the wrist.

He looked surprised, and then delighted.

"Well done, child. You may be capable of working your will on the world after all." He picked up the bloody, green-splattered hand and pushed it back into place, smoothing skin over the cut as though sculpting with clay. "But you will grow weary eventually, and I will not. Another bout?"

He saluted again.

Rosa had already relit the candle.

"Isabelle Barron," she said, "be remembered. I invite you in."

26

THE COPPER BARRIER CRACKED. FOG CAME BILLOWING through like a breaking wave. It flattened the militia and their mopeds, shocked summertime trees into scarlet colors, and flowed wide around Jasper's circle.

Figures moved through the fog. Long-limbed and towering things came striding by. Smaller things came skittering. Spirits made new clothes for themselves from dirt, leaves, and whatever else they found.

The militia screamed, flailed, and lashed out with their weapons—just as Nell had said they would. Random bursts of flame from Humphrey blossomed in the fog. Firelight glinted on Englebert's huge, goofy spear with his every desperate swing.

Well, now they're distracted. Jasper thought. He held his quarterstaff in his right hand, took up the candle with his left, and stepped outside his circle.

The noise of ten thousand voices became instantly louder, overwhelming his ears. The air stole warmth from his goosebumped skin.

Englebert came at him. Maybe he recognized Jasper. Maybe he just swung at everything that moved. Either way, the older boy held his pole-arm entirely wrong. Jasper whacked it aside.

"Ow, ow, ow," Englebert cried out as he dropped the weapon, hands stinging.

Ghosts came at Jasper. Some were in pain and lashed out at the living. Others were made out of pain. He spun his copper-tipped staff and kept them back. He pressed on, upstream against the flow of cold, haunted fog.

A guard threw a knife at him, which was ridiculous. Jasper could juggle four knives and a vase of flowers. He dropped the candle, caught the knife, and then scooped the candle back up before it hit the ground.

The knife felt solid and expensive. He decided to keep it, tucked it in his belt, and pushed on.

Here, close to the barrier and beside the breach, ghosts and spirits screamed as they passed through. Jasper couldn't sort out joy from rage inside that noise, or whether or not he made it himself.

He slammed the candle down. It blocked the flow of fog.

"Not so fast," he tried to say, but his own throat was raw and scratched. "Not so fast," he tried again. "Come home. You're invited. Just don't crush us all when you get here."

He dug in his pockets for the chantey-etched Zippo.

It wasn't there. Sugar cubes and salt packets spilled out, but no lighter. He couldn't find the lighter. It must have fallen from his pocket somewhere between this spot and the fairgrounds.

Jasper's heart sank all the way down to his heels. Then he stood, turned, and waved both hands.

"Huuuuumphreeeeeeeeeeeey!" he called out, voice ghostly and menacing.

Humphrey yelped somewhere nearby and cut loose with the flamethrower.

Jasper dropped, rolled, and tried to get out of the way.

Barron tried to blow the candle out again, but it was too late. Isabelle came through. She made herself a shape from scattered leaves and dust.

The old man seemed to shrivel. "I let you go," he whined. "I set you free. Why aren't you gone?"

"Remember me," said Isabelle. Rosa heard her

mother's voice alongside the crunch of dead leaves rustling together. "I have no portraits pasted up in every public lobby to keep me known, and keep me whole. But my hand painted that first portrait, the one that still hangs in our home. You will remember."

"Of course I remember," Barron said, but he would not look at her.

She stepped up to the inside edge of Rosa's half-circle. Her gown of leaves swirled in a whirlwind at her feet. Rosa tried to keep out of her way.

"You cut a wound in the world and made the world forget that it was ever there," Isabelle went on. "But it festers."

"No," he rasped. "No. I built a town. A beautiful, prosperous town. With wealth from the mine I built it. Now I keep it free and unburdened."

"The mine poisoned half of our wells. We died for your metal. I died for your metal. But the survivors honor you. They only know how to remember half of you."

"Why won't you leave?" Barron demanded and begged. "Why can't I make you leave?" He lashed out with his rusting foil. Rosa ducked. The sword passed through the dust and leaves of Isabelle, but she remained. Then she raised her arm. This clearly took effort. It looked as if she didn't remember how limbs worked when they still had bones inside.

Rosa scuffed away the line of her half-circle with one foot to let the ghost cross.

Please work, please work, please work, she thought. *He's afraid of you. Just you. Nothing else. He hardly even notices anything else.*

"Remember me," Isabelle said, her voice a soft scrape of dry leaves. She put one hand to Barron's chest.

He sighed as though relieved. Then he burned.

Rosa looked away from the heat and the eye-searing brightness. When she looked back, scorched bones lay scattered where Bartholomew Theosophras Barron used to be.

Isabelle slowly turned the dust and leaves of her makeshift face to consider Rosa.

"You're welcome," Rosa said.

You owe me, is what she meant. *You took my mother's voice. She needs it back.*

Isabelle said nothing. The whirlwind of her gown grew stronger. Then she was gone, dust and leaves scattering on their way down the mountain and into town.

Mist flowed like smoke from the candle flame. Other ghosts began to pass through on their own way home.

27

JASPER ROLLED ACROSS THE GROUND TO CONVINCE himself, and his clothes, that they were not burning. They didn't seem to be burning. He rolled one more time, just to make sure. Then he glanced at the candle. One whole side looked slick and half-melted, but the wick was lit.

Fog glowed around the candle flame.

Voices billowed through it and murmured to each other.

Jasper listened. He stood up. He stood very still.

The militia scattered, but Jasper was only vaguely aware of them. He was far more conscious of unseen fingers that brushed against his own. Small things at his feet made legs from sticks, and ran. A great lumbering and invisible something came up to him. Jasper couldn't see what it was, but he felt an awkward impatience from it, so he stepped sideways to let it pass. The lumbering something went away downhill, into town.

"Welcome home," Jasper said, his heart full of a feeling that he didn't have a name for, one he had always missed but never knew was missing. He wondered how much of home he would recognize once he hiked back down through the foothills. He wanted to find out. But he couldn't bring himself to leave. Not just yet. "Welcome home," he said again, to everything around him.

Hoof beats struck the ground—sudden, close, and getting closer. Jasper tensed and tried to sort out which direction a horse might be coming from. He tried to make sure that he wouldn't be trampled by it. But the beat of those hooves sounded confident rather than skittish.

Jerónimo trotted up and whinnied low.

He was not himself. Not only himself. He was now a haunted thing made out of smooth, riverworn stones piled up into a horse-shaped cairn. But he still wore his old saddle, and his stone hooves stamped out an impatient invitation.

Jasper didn't feel too confident about riding a haunted horse. But riding did beat walking. He mounted up, careful not to touch Jerónimo with any of the copper that he wore or carried. He half expected the horse to lose his shape and scatter like a thousand dropped marbles. But he also half expected the horse to stay whole, and *that* half turned out to be right.

Jerónimo tossed his head and trotted down the mountainside.

The forest around them slowly woke to its own haunting.

Rosa hiked northward and down.

Jasper rode southward on a haunted horse.

They met on Isabelle Road beside the fairgrounds.

"Hey," he said.

"Hey," she answered, equally relieved. "Nice ride."

"Thanks." Jasper dismounted. "This is Jerónimo. I think. A piece of him, anyway."

The cold, stone steed stamped against the road, impatient. Jasper offered a sugar cube. Jerónimo took it, but crunched granules of sugar fell back out of his mouth, *through* his mouth, and scattered on the ground. He stamped again and sidled up sideways, still asking for something.

"What is it?" Jasper asked. "Is it the saddle? You've worn that since yesterday. Probably feels raw. Even though yesterday you were made out of other stuff."

He couldn't unbuckle the straps. The buckles had rusted together as though weeks and months had passed instead of a single day. Jasper took his new knife and cut all the straps loose. Jerónimo was already moving by the time his saddle hit the ground. Jasper and Rosa watched him gallop away.

"I think it worked," Jasper said, his voice guarded, still unsure what their victory might mean.

"I think maybe it did," Rosa said. "Any trouble at your end?"

"A little. I had to fight my way through the living." He spun the quarterstaff once around his wrist.

"Lucky you. I had to duel with the dead."

"Don't you *prefer* the dead for company?"

"Shut up," she said. "Not always."

Floating lights filled the dusk like whole galaxies of fireflies. Actual fireflies stayed low in the grass and blinked anxious messages to each other.

"What are those?" Jasper whispered.

"Wisps," she told him.

He had heard of wisps. "The kind that lead travelers off-road to get lost?"

"No," Rosa said. "Not really. You'd probably get disoriented if you followed one around, but that isn't the wisp's fault. They're lost, too. We should make a bunch of lanterns, just to give them somewhere to be. But . . ."

"But what?"

"But I've never seen so many," she admitted. "We'd need a lot of candles."

Larger things moved through the trees. Some of them were made out of trees. Others made shapes for themselves out of mud and moss.

"This is going to get interesting," Rosa said. "And messy. Come on. Let's find our parents. A piece of my mom is still missing."

28

THE INGOT RENAISSANCE FESTIVAL STOOD IN
silence. No power tools hummed. No hammers struck.
No one sang.

Jasper and Rosa picked their way through the
half-repaired wreckage of the wall. Everyone else held
themselves very still and watched the ghosts return.

A lute string sounded. Someone picked out a tune,
one long note at a time.

Rosa spotted Uncle Fox. The musician still sat at
the base of his tree, surrounded now by dozens of listening wisps.

Jasper pointed to where his parents stood together, hand
in hand. He went to stand beside them. Rosa followed.

"This is something to see," Sir Dad whispered. His voice sounded hesitant and ordinary, stripped of the accent that he loved to use. "But I'm sorry to see it. We're done. This festival is over. Great, big, fantastical reenactment just can't win an argument against history. Not when the real thing decides to rise up."

Jasper swallowed. The sound of his throat sounded loud in his ears. *I did this*, he thought. *I helped do this. We ended the unhaunting of Ingot. On purpose.*

"Maybe it can," he said. "Somehow. We'll figure it out." He put on the accent his father had dropped. "This is the largest and most splendid celebration of its kind to be found anywhere in the world."

Sir Dad gave Jasper's shoulder an awkward, affectionate pat.

"Have you seen my mom?" Rosa asked. "You haven't met her, but she looks like me. Almost exactly like me. Except taller. I left her with Nell."

"They'll be near Nell's shop, I imagine," said Mrs. Chevalier. She stared at a tongue of blue flame as it danced above the chimney of the Tacky Tavern. Then she shook her head as though shaking off daydreams. "Over that way."

"I know the way to Nell's shop, Mom," Jasper said.

"Be careful, son," she said, but she didn't sound worried. The thing Ingot feared most had already

William Alexander

happened. Now both of Jasper's parents watched the haunted festival as though it was burning to the ground around them—bright, beautiful, and ending forever.

We'll figure this out, Jasper promised again. *We will.*

Rosa tugged his arm. They found Nell fussing around outside her shop. Athena Díaz stood beside her, arms crossed and eyes wide. She smiled. Hers might have been the only smiling face in Ingot.

"Specialist!" Nell called out when she caught sight of Rosa. "Two poltergeists are playing catch with my knives. On the ceiling. Standing on the ceiling. I'm pretty sure they're poltergeists, anyway."

"Long arms?" Rosa asked. "Large eyes? Short legs? Only visible when you glance at them sideways?"

She spoke to Nell, but watched her mother. They shared a look. That look meant something, it had to mean something, but whatever it was remained voiceless. Rosa held their eye contact carefully, worried that it might break and desperately wanting to know what it meant.

"Yes," Nell said. "All of those things."

Rosa nodded without looking away from her mother. "Poltergeists. Definitely."

"They are throwing my knives around."

"Try not to distract them, then," Rosa suggested. "Or stand under them."

"Thanks so very much," Nell growled back at

170

her. "If I'd known you were bringing all of this down on us, I might have been less helpful. Right now Mousetrap is reenacting old shows that its floorboards remember. Glass trinkets are melting in the glassware shop. The practice swords in the prop cabinet are rattling."

"They probably want to practice," Rosa said. "How's my mom?"

Nell's voice softened. "She's been like this. Perked up and grinned just as soon as the ghosts came rolling home. But not a word from her."

"She doesn't have any words," Rosa said. "She doesn't have a voice. But I just returned it to the library, so I think we can find it there."

Mom turned right around and walked away.

Rosa and Jasper went after her.

Nell followed in their wake, even though she grumbled about how much she did not *want* to chase them through whatever fresh mess they might create next.

Athena Díaz led them all through the festival and its parking lot. She left their family car behind, which was probably for the best. Rosa could hear haunted things happening inside its engine.

The small procession made its way into town, into the very center of the broken circle that surrounded Ingot.

29

BOOKS RUSTLED THEIR PAGES IN THE STACKS. IT sounded like applause, or maybe warm rain in the distance. It sounded familiar. Rosa closed her eyes and savored that sound.

She also heard a noise like thunder coming from somewhere behind the main desk, but she decided to ignore that for the moment.

"Where should we look for Isabelle Barron?" Jasper whispered. "Upstairs? I bet she's upstairs."

Rosa nodded. "I'm guessing so. That room has changed the least since this place became a library." She led them to Special Collections.

The door was locked.

"I bet we could just break this door down," Rosa said. "We're supposed to respect boundaries. But I bet we could."

Mrs. Jillynip came fretting at them. Fierce eyebrows rode high on her forehead. "Please do not break anything. There is quite enough chaos and unrest already. The books are reshelving themselves according to some whimsical system that I don't understand. The interlibrary loan materials are absolutely riotous. Neighbors I buried years ago are here to reread their favorites. Small lights are floating in the rafters. Things that I cannot look at directly are playing catch with my DISCONTINUED stamps. And the coffeemaker in the break room seems to have . . . awakened. It's unhappy about something. I can't understand the thundering growls that it makes."

"Ah," Rosa said. "That's what that noise is."

"It's loud," Mrs. Jillynip complained. She seemed almost tearful. "I can't get it to quiet down. I don't know what to do."

"I'll talk to it," Rosa promised. "It probably wants a respectful tribute."

"Thank you, child."

"But first we need to go upstairs. Would you please unlock the door?"

Mrs. Jillynip's eyebrows shot up higher. "Are all of you going through?"

"Yes," Rosa said.

"I trust that you will not handle any of the materials in Special Collections. Not without the proper gloves. Not without signing the clipboard." She said "clipboard" as if it were a talisman that could protect her collection from every bad thing. Maybe it was.

"Of course," Rosa promised. "No handling. We're just passing through. We have business upstairs with the lady of the house."

"I see," Mrs. Jillynip said, though she said it in a way that meant *I do not see what you mean, and I would rather not, so please go about your business without explaining it to me.*

She unlocked the door. Rosa led the way through. Mrs. Jillynip closed and locked the door again behind them. Nell flinched at the rattle and click.

Scraping, scratching, wailing noises came down the spiral staircase.

"Are you sure we should go up there?" Nell asked. "We should maybe consider *not* going up there."

Athena climbed the stairs.

"We'll be fine," Rosa said. "We've got Mom."

There was a wind in the upstairs apartment. It disturbed clouds of dust from the floor and the furniture. It tore Barron's map of Ingot into pieces. Those pieces swirled in a whirlwind. Dust and paper took the shape of Isabelle's gown.

She moved through the room, agitated, picking things up and then setting them down again. The living stood together at the top of the stairs. The dead ignored them until Athena Díaz stepped forward, reached out, and took Isabelle's hand.

"Hello," she said with her own voice.

Isabelle snatched the hand free. It dissolved. She remade it from the dust she disturbed.

Rosa's mom took the hand again. "Hello."

Isabelle tore away. She tore herself in half and then reshaped herself in the farthest corner of the room.

"This place is mine." The ghost spoke through clenched teeth made of ink-stained paper. "This voice is mine."

Mom moved forward.

Isabelle held up her arm, palm outward like a barrier. She had pressed that palm against Mr. Barron's chest right before she reduced him to a pile of smoking bones.

Rosa drew her sword, suddenly unsure that her mother could handle this. But Mom reached out, took the ghost's threatening hand for the third time, and held on.

"Hello," she said. "That's my voice you've borrowed."

Isabelle drew herself up. She grew taller. Old possessions fell from shelves and shattered against the floor. The wind picked up their pieces and used them to give more substance to the towering ghost.

"Mom?" Rosa whispered, too softly to be heard over the swirling, shrieking noise.

Her mother maintained her grip. "Take a moment to collect yourself," she said, loud but without shouting. "This tantrum is unworthy of you."

"How dare you intrude?" The ghost took up even more space with the booming sound of her borrowed voice.

"You are in my house now," the specialist said. "I live here. My daughter lives here. We can make you welcome here. We can honor your memory, and your memories. Are you prepared to earn that respect?"

Isabelle grew larger. The wind howled louder. "I will not be silenced again."

"Then borrow my voice when you need it," Mom offered. "But I will have it back now."

The two stared each other down. Rosa clenched her grip on the hilt of her sword. Then she loosened that grip, just a little, to stay nimble and fight-ready.

Nell put a hand on Rosa's shoulder. "I think she's got this, kiddo."

The ghost diminished. The whirlwind of her gown

stopped howling. She bent her arm and wrist as though expecting Athena to kiss her hand, and glared as though expecting Athena to burst into flame.

"I accept," Isabelle said.

"Welcome home," said the specialist.

The wind held its breath. Scraps of paper, shards of glass, and swirling dust all hit the floor.

Mom dusted off her hands.

"Is anyone else hungry?" she asked. "I need to eat something more than a stale bagel and a tasteless turkey leg."

Rosa dropped her sword and nearly knocked her mother over with a tackle hug.

30

MOST OF THE RESTAURANTS IN INGOT HAD ALREADY shut down in their sudden panic. Every one of them was haunted now, and few knew how to handle that. But Nell's favorite burger place, the Tiny Diner, employed a chef from out of town. He remembered how to properly appease unhappy ovens, and the waitress knew to set an extra plate at every booth and table. The diner stayed open.

Rosa kind of liked this place. Every booth had its own personal jukebox bolted to the wall. Theirs sported a handwritten OUT OF ORDER sign, but it still hummed off-key to itself.

The food turned out to be decent. Not as good

as the restaurants on Eat Street, two blocks south of Rosa's old library in the city, but still decent. Both Rosa and Jasper neglected to chew and practically inhaled face-size burgers whole. Then they slurped milkshakes through thick straws.

Rosa elbowed her mother in the ribs.

"Hey! What was that for?"

"Nothing," Rosa mumbled around the straw. Then she did it again, just to hear Mom protest again, just to make sure that she still could.

Nell insisted on paying the tab, and on walking Jasper home afterward. "I need to see how your folks are holding up," she said. "I also need make certain that you don't get stepped on by trees between here and there."

Jasper was concerned about his parents, but not at all worried about walking trees. He waved at Rosa. "See you."

"See you," she said. "If your household spirits don't let you sleep, try stacking a pile of pebbles under the bed. They like piles of pebbles. And I can come talk to them tomorrow."

Jasper nodded. "Pebbles. Got it."

He could have said more. He wanted to say more. *We did it. We saved this place. Or maybe we didn't save it, because everything is different now. I'm still glad. The town is dead. Long live the town.* But he didn't say any of it. He felt too stuffed full of burger and milkshake. Besides, he knew that Rosa understood.

The squire and the blacksmith walked away in the evening wisp light.

The two appeasement specialists went home to their library. They heard screaming along the way.

"Should we check in on that?" Rosa asked.

"Nope," her mother said. "Bedtime. And those sounded like screams of annoyance to me. No danger. No distress. They can wait. We'll have plenty of work to do in the morning."

She sounded tired. But she did not sound weary, defeated, or in any way haunted, and her voice belonged to her own purposeful self.

Rosa took her mother's hand and said nothing loudly.

Once home they moved the couch so as not to climb over it. Contagious yawns passed back and forth between them. Mom sprinkled a little sage into the kitchen sink to keep the garbage disposal from grumbling, and then she smiled and said good night as though the day had been ordinary.

Rosa closed her bedroom door.

She opened the curtains over her window mural and watched as a wind swayed the painted trees.

She listened to her bedspread, a quilt patched together from other, older blankets, as it murmured in mismatched fragments of lullabies and bedtime stories.

Her familiar belongings stirred inside cardboard boxes, remembering themselves.

"I'll unpack tomorrow," Rosa told them. "I promise."

ACKNOWLEDGMENTS

A *Properly Unhaunted Place* owes its existence to the help and support of these magnificent people:

Alice Dodge; Peter S. Beagle; Kekla Magoon; Karen Meisner; Rio Saito; Leah Schwartz; Nathan Clough; Ivan Bialostosky; Elise Matthesen; Haddayr Copley-Woods; David Schwartz; Stacy Thieszen; Barth Anderson; Sara Logan; Bethany Aronoff; Jon Stockdale; Melon Wedick; the Larsons Evan, Bryce, and Shelley; the blacksmiths at Oakeshott; the scholarship of Ken Mondschein; and the professional excellence of Barry Goldblatt, Tricia Ready, Annie Nybo, and Karen Wojtyla.

Raise a glass.

WITHDRAWN